Ordinary Justice

Ordinary Justice

Trudy Labovitz

Spinsters Ink
Duluth, MN, USA

Ordinary Justice © 1999 by Trudy Labovitz

First edition published May 1999 by Spinsters Ink
10-9-8-7-6-5-4-3-2-1

Spinsters Ink
32 E. First St., #330
Duluth, MN 55802-2002 USA

Cover illustration by Celeste Gallup Laub
Cover design by Sara Sinnard, Sarin Creative

Production:

Liz Brissett	Claire Kirch
Charlene Brown	Jean Nygaard
Helen Dooley	Kim Riordan
Joan Drury	Emily Soltis
Tracy Gilsvik	Amy Strasheim
Marian Hunstiger	Liz Tufte
Kelly Kager	Nancy Walker

Library of Congress Cataloging-in-Publication Data
Labovitz, Trudy, 1954–
   Ordinary justice / Trudy Labovitz. — 1st ed.
     p.   cm.
   ISBN 1-883523-31-1 (alk. paper)
   1. Private investigators—West Virginia—Fiction.
   2. Women detectives—West Virginia—Fiction.
   I. Title
   PS3562.A235507   1999
   813'.54—dc21   99–19045
                                              CIP

Printed in the USA on recycled paper with soy-based ink

Acknowledgments

Very special thanks to Celeste Gallup Laub for suffering through every iteration of this manuscript (and others), for the beautiful painting on the cover (and all the others), and for her unwavering, steadfast friendship and encouragement.

Thanks, too, for their ongoing encouragement and generosity, to Celeste and Kelly McWhirter, Cele Bonomo, Carol Fryday and Dan Kamin, and last but not least, Debbie Bailey and family, who also handed me a Mac just when I needed it. A person couldn't have better friends.

I am so very grateful to Joan Drury and Kelly Kager (and everyone at Spinsters), who knew just how to shovel through the muck to find the good stuff.

For their silent encouragement, their loyalty and support, and their unstinting love, my heartfelt thanks to Kaylo, Mischa, Dickens, Seeger, and you, too, Meadow.

Dedication

For my mom, who has always believed.

And in memory of my dad
and Taj.

Zoe straightened to ease the ache in the small of her back. Digging potatoes from the garden was a task Zoe had not done since childhood. She had forgotten the sweat it entailed. This was the first season she had planted potatoes, and she had come up with a surprisingly good crop, especially considering the condition of the soil when she had first moved in, almost three years earlier.

As she leaned on the garden fork and proudly surveyed the mounds of dirty spuds now littering the ground, a movement from up the hillside caught her eye. Someone was cautiously picking her way down through the overgrowth.

The farm behind Zoe's had been abandoned for years. That had counted as a plus in her decision to buy this place. Isolation was what Zoe had craved. She had been on the run from Washington, D.C., from her former job, and from anyone who might have a tie to her former life. That no one was likely pursuing her had little to do with it.

Zoe's house stood at the end of a wooded, mile-long semiprivate road. Only the gas company shared access. On the far side of the driveway was a steep mountainside with a river at the bottom. Beyond the house and garden, scrub and wasteland surrounded worked-out coal mines that were sealed against the entry of people and the exit of acid drainage.

The only real access that she could not control came from the hillside behind the house, where the George farm butted up against her land. When Zoe moved in, she had checked out the place once or twice a month, in the interests of curiosity, safety, and, she knew, semiunreasonable fear. She could not shake the feeling that bullets could come from any direction, that anyone could be cut down without warning.

Despite the seeming ease with which she had slipped into this life, seeing someone walk down from among the trees shook Zoe's complacency. She had again grown used to the slower pace of the West Virginia hills and had settled back into a cushiony time much like her childhood, when responsibilities were minimal and freedom beckoned at every corner. The stranger's appearance now negated that idyll, showed it up for a sham.

A quivering began again in her stomach, and she knew the hands on the garden fork had started to shake.

Three years ago, Zoe's best friend, Karen O'Malley, had been gunned down by her estranged husband, Paul Martin. He had ambushed them from the porch of Zoe's D.C. condominium. In turn, and seconds too late to save Karen, Zoe had shot him. Paul Martin still had a brother in northern Virginia, as well as one or two friends who had not been as quick as the law in declaring his death a justifiable homicide. Who was to say that the person now approaching had nothing to do with them?

Her friend's death was the main cause of her disquiet, but Zoe also knew she had made one or two enemies while she had conducted investigations for the Justice Department; she had received a few threats from that territory as well. She felt her paranoia was not completely misplaced.

Before the woman drew dangerously closer, Zoe measured the distance to the house. A quick sprint might get her safely inside. The basement was below ground, where bullets couldn't reach.

But each second of delay brought the stranger nearer. Zoe tried to give the appearance of nonchalance, even while her hands tightened around the garden fork. If necessary, she would use it as a weapon of defense.

The woman stopped at the edge of the garden. She wore dusty jeans and a faded denim jacket. Her light brown hair was pulled back in a loose ponytail. Tentatively raising a hand in greeting, she attempted a shy smile.

Zoe kept hold of the garden fork but relaxed the death grip she had on the implement. She pasted on a smile of her own and nodded in welcome as she stepped over rows of late beans in order to approach the woman.

"Hi, I'm Zoe Kergulin. I didn't realize anyone had moved in next door, or I would have been over to say hello."

"Hi, Zoe. Pleased to meet you. I'm Susan R—." Her lips formed an 'R' by habit, but she stopped further sound before it left her mouth. She smiled again, embarrassed and momentarily panicked.

Zoe watched as the woman fought to regain self-control.

"I'm Susan." She repeated, nodding, deciding the first name was enough. "Susan. I'm renting the mobile home up there. The house looks like it was nice once, but I don't think it's livable anymore."

"Not even for raccoons and rats," Zoe agreed.

Susan nervously surveyed Zoe's three-story Queen Anne. Her eye traveled over the towers and chimneys, studied the many windows filled with stained glass, and lingered on the huge porch.

Restlessly, her hands searched her jeans pocket. She tugged at her jacket. Her feet scuffed the dirt.

"This your house?" she asked. Nodding in response to Zoe's affirmative answer, Susan added, "The real estate agent said a woman owned the house down the mountain, but she sure didn't tell me it looked like this. I've never seen anything like it."

"She's a late Victorian," Zoe said proudly, relaxing for the first time as she admired her house. Objectively, she knew the paint was peeling, the shutters rotting, and the detailed woodwork falling apart, but her eye saw none of that.

"It's nice," Susan said, her attention already diverted. Her glance traveled up the long drive and then again around the garden. Back in the front pockets of her jeans, her hands made fists.

"I was wondering if maybe you could give me a lift into Beverage tomorrow, if you're going." Susan kept her eyes on the ground where the tines of the garden fork rested. "My van broke down, and I had to leave it at the service station and walk back."

"You need a ride to DeSoto's?" It was the only gas station in town. "Sure. I'd be glad to. I'll be home all day tomorrow, so whenever it's ready . . ."

"Actually," Susan stammered, "I don't have a phone yet, so I can't check when the car will be finished. If you could just drop me there sometime late in the day, I'm sure that would be fine."

"How about some potatoes?" Zoe asked, beginning to stroll toward her harvest. It was the first time she had turned her back on the woman. "I planted way more than I'll be able to use."

"Oh, I couldn't—" Susan began to say, but stopped herself. She squared her shoulders. "I'd sure appreciate that."

As Zoe loaded one of the bags she'd brought out, she cocked her head. "How about staying for dinner?"

A genuine smile leapt to the face of the younger woman. "Thank you. The stove works fine up in that trailer, but it's electric, and there's not even a microwave, and I don't know how—"

The burst of a police car siren briefly pierced the air, swiftly followed by the sound of tires hitting potholes on the ungraded driveway. A dust cloud rose among the trees, and in front of it appeared a white sheriff's car. The emergency lights flashed a couple of times.

Zoe shook her head even as she smiled. "My cousin, Ethan McKenna," she said by way of explanation. "He always needs to announce himself." But as she turned to share what she hoped would be a moment of female communion with Susan, she saw instead that the color had drained from the other woman's face. A smudge that looked like dirt, but was probably the last trace of a bruise, suddenly stood out plainly on Susan's cheek.

"I've got to go," Susan said. "Thanks again for the potatoes. I'll be by tomorrow afternoon."

By the time Ethan had maneuvered through the turnaround and pointed his car back up the drive, Susan had already disappeared into the trees.

Sliding from the Blazer, Ethan raised a questioning eyebrow in Zoe's direction. She shrugged in response, even as she grinned at his arrival.

The first summer she had spent on her aunt and uncle's farm, when she was six and Ethan was eight, she had fallen in love with him. Five summers later, when she had confided her secret longing for one of the seasonal workers, Ethan had allowed back that he, too, had a crush on the young man. That had marked the end of Zoe's plans to marry her cousin but the beginning of a deeper understanding between them.

Growing up, Ethan had attempted to fit in, and Zoe had never betrayed him. Even when he'd married, she had kept her counsel and wished him well. Now that he was divorced and on the verge of accepting himself, Zoe was excited about what might lie ahead for him.

As he sauntered over to the large garden, Ethan gazed up the mountainside where Susan had disappeared and said, "I did take a shower before work today, Zoe."

"It wasn't that she got a whiff of the McKenna charm, Ethan. She was terrified as soon as she saw the car. Maybe as soon as she heard the siren."

"Want me to run her name?" He gestured back toward his car.

Zoe shook her head. "I don't know it anyway. She got as far as Susan R-r-r-r."

"Got a dog in your throat?"

Zoe smiled in spite of herself, but her eyes kept returning up the mountainside. "It's probably nothing. There's probably a collection agency after her."

"The college loan people, most likely."

"Could be Girl Scouts coming to repossess cookies she didn't pay for."

"Maybe she tore the tag off her mattress. And robbed a bank."

"Or it's a boyfriend or husband." They sobered and exchanged a quick hug and kiss. Zoe shrugged off the momentary gloom. "Tomorrow I'm taking her into Beverage so she can pick up her car at DeSoto's. Maybe she'll let me know more then."

"I didn't realize there was anyone up on that farm. Isn't the old woman dead?"

"Yeah, but her kids have been trying to rent out the trailer for a couple of years now, while they work out how to divvy up the property. Meanwhile, the house is falling down. There are more shingles on the ground than on the roof. And the back porch caved in sometime over the summer."

"You've been up there regularly?" He asked offhandedly, but his eyes studied her intently. He could guess why she kept surveying the farm.

"Just to pay social calls now," Zoe smiled crookedly.

Ethan eased an arm around his cousin's shoulders and gave her a quick squeeze. Empathy with how Zoe was coming to terms with the circumstances of her friend's murder was one of Ethan's strong points. It had been his immediate understanding that had drawn her back to Bickle County when she'd needed to retreat somewhere.

"Hey, look at all these spuds!" Ethan enthused.

Zoe took a deep breath. She determined to question Susan further, check out whether she truly was alone at that trailer, and find out if she had any connections to the D.C. area. Hoping that would be enough to settle her head and her stomach, Zoe thought that maybe it would help Susan as well.

"Did you grow up around here?" Zoe asked as she picked her way between the boulders and gullies that characterized her driveway. She took her eyes from the road for just a second to watch Susan's reaction.

Susan nodded. "Not too far away."

"Same here," Zoe allowed. "My brothers and sisters and I used to come to Bickle County every summer to visit, so moving here was like coming home. Have you ever lived anywhere else?"

"Here and there," Susan replied, and pointedly gazed out the car window.

"Ever been outside of West Virginia?" Zoe tried again. Susan seemed to be as closemouthed about personal details as Zoe was.

"Just to sightsee or vacation," Susan said.

Zoe nodded. She was beginning to believe that Susan had no connections to her former life.

"You ever been married?" Susan asked abruptly.

"No." At the top of the driveway, Zoe turned right onto the pavement. When she stepped on the gas, the car responded immediately.

When Zoe added no elaboration, Susan nodded. "Smart. Say, do you know of any place that's looking for someone? I thought maybe that college in Russell Creek might be looking for a secretary, or maybe . . . I don't know. I wasn't planning on having the van break down, that's all."

"I don't know of anyone who's hiring now, but I'll keep my eyes open." Zoe slowed as they approached the turn onto the main road into town. "Have you ever been married, Susan?"

"Hasn't just about everyone? Hey, over there. That's my van."

The thing had once been a tan color, but now it was mostly rust. The rear window was clouded with oil that had chugged out of the tailpipe. As Zoe ran her hand through the air in response to Susan's wave of thanks and dismissal, she could see that the van's windshield was duct-taped to the frame.

With a final glance, Zoe turned left out of the station and headed for an evening security seminar she was teaching in-house for a company in Russell Creek.

When Zoe had first returned to West Virginia, Ethan had encouraged her to acquire her private investigator's license. It had given her a starting point to launch her new career. Her experience with the Justice Department had more than qualified her for the role. But she had deliberately devoted her skills to security work for corporations, installing protocols and training personnel. In truth, she had spent most of her time not being a private investigator. Now, as she drove, she found herself reviewing, sifting, and turning over all that she knew about Susan and the George farm.

Later that night when she returned home, Zoe clocked the distance from the garage to her house. Three and two-tenths miles. Susan's trailer was at least a mile farther on, maybe two, if she'd stuck strictly to the road. After her car had broken down, had Susan walked the entire way looking for whomever she was running from to show up, either around the next bend or the last one?

Zoe saw Susan again the next day, when the younger woman dropped off a loaf of freshly baked potato bread. She came into the house and made a fuss over Zoe's three cats but did not stay longer than it took to again thank her benefactor for the ride. Susan's eyes kept straying out the window, her feet stepping toward the door.

Zoe made a point of saying, "Susan, whatever I can do for you, I'd sure be glad to—"

"Thanks again for the potatoes," Susan said, interrupting with a nervous showing of teeth that passed for a smile. She hurried out the door. "If I don't get up that hillside before dark, I'll probably wander around in the wilderness for years."

"I'll be glad to drive you back."

"No, thanks. I really do enjoy the walk." She had no phone so could not call to let Zoe know she had arrived safely, nor could Zoe buzz her to relay how much she enjoyed the bread.

As she went through her days, Zoe thought about Susan and wondered how she was doing, but the work and the house kept her occupied, so it was not until almost a week later that she hiked up a craggy hillside toward the George farm.

Leaves were already crunching underfoot, although the trees still blazed brilliant with crimsons and golds. It had been raining on and off all day, but the bright foliage made it seem as if the sun wrapped the world in its glow.

There was no path to the George place. Zoe made her way as she went, passing little piles of deer droppings, watching birds swoop low, and even spotting a fox slinking silently into the shadows. Aside from slipping once while crossing the creek that supplied her water, she uneventfully climbed the hill. Unbidden, images of her childhood flashed through her mind. Then, she had worn no sturdy shoes, and her jacket had been threadbare with wear. Her family had been poor, but as the sixth child, the oldest of the youngest group, her mother always said, she had been coddled and well-loved. Need was a concept she had not learned from living; dawning understanding of the extent of her family's poverty had come from the multitude of books she swallowed whole back then.

Next, Zoe had to cross the old pasture, where burrs stuck like lint to her sweater, and then the barnyard, where the barn had long since burned down, but the mud still lingered. As always, she stopped and surveyed the ruin of the farmhouse from the cover of a hedge before passing behind it. Nothing had changed. Boards still blinded the windows, and padlocks fettered the doors.

Another overgrown meadow had to be crossed before Zoe saw the short line of pines that stretched above the trailer. Susan's rusty van was parked beside the propane tank.

It looked very peaceful. As she drew nearer, Zoe could see what she took for geraniums blooming in the kitchen window. The thought that Susan was making the place her own, that the flowers were her way of declaring her presence, made Zoe start to relax, to entertain the idea of a new friendship blossoming along with the potted plant.

Only when she got very close did she realize that it was not geraniums she had been admiring. Handprints in dried bloodstains dotted the inside of the window. There were no potted flowers at all.

Feeling the still-familiar rush of adrenaline mixing with the paralysis of fear, Zoe dropped to a crouch behind a tree and concentrated her senses, her eyes focused on the trailer. The front door was dented, hanging lopsided from only one hinge. Adrenaline and need to know won out over fear and tension, and she slowly crept forward, hugging the dirt until she could press her back against the cold metal siding of the trailer. Her heart hammered like the bass on a car radio.

She spotted a baseball bat in pieces on the ground just outside the door. Straining her ears for the slightest breath, she heard only the swishing and sighing of the wind through the leaves.

She figured whatever had happened was over, but it was foolish to take chances. With a lunge and a whirl, Zoe burst through the doorway, still keeping low. It took a moment for her eyes to adjust to the twilight inside, for her brain to register that the form on the floor beside the bed was a quilt and not a body.

She inched her way to a standing position and slowly took in the destruction around her. The place was empty of life. No smells littered the air; no movement caught her eye. She stepped out of her shoes and slowly walked up and down the narrow central hallway, careful to keep her hands in her pockets, sidling almost comically to avoid touching the double wedding ring quilt. It seemed, miraculously, to have escaped destruction. With eyes and nose and ears, she searched high and low, but there was no evidence that Susan was still there. The dried stains on the window remained the only blood she saw.

Back at the door, she slipped awkwardly into her shoes without untying them and then circled the house twice, once close to the trailer, and then again in a larger circumference, searching for an injured woman. Or a dead one. But she found nothing.

Only then did she break into a run and head back across the meadow toward home and a phone. Rain began pelting down, making the ground slippery and the footing treacherous, but still she pushed her pace. It was true that Susan could have been missing for days, but maybe it had only been minutes, despite the dried appearance of the blood. If so, time was of the essence.

It took three tries before she could unlock the front door. It was Susan who had been in trouble all along, Susan who was most likely the victim of violence. Zoe had let her fears for her own safety overtake her reason.

The thought that Susan might be days gone did not stop the

panic that tickled at her stomach or lessen the shaking of her hand. She used the speed dial. For once, she got right through to her cousin.

"Ethan!" It wasn't until she heard her own voice that she realized her anger was, in a large part, self-directed. "Damn it, Ethan! He took her!"

Her name was Susan Rourke. Zoe had called DeSoto's and talked to Jack LaSalle, the mechanic who kept her old Chevy on the road. At the same time, Ethan had checked with the real estate agent who had rented out the trailer. Both sources agreed on the woman's name. It was Chickie Ondean, one of Ethan's deputies, who had found Susan's home address on the owner's card in the van.

When the police went to the cinder block home in Sinksville to question Susan's husband, they found him gone. He hadn't been to work in days, mail had piled up in his box, and his pickup truck was missing.

The following morning, Zoe stepped out of her car in Sinksville, an old mining town almost as small as Beverage but still much larger than the hollow where she had grown up. The place sat high in a saddle in the mountains, surrounded by second growth forest and campgrounds. A recently opened historical trail bisected the area, and tourism had replaced mining as the main industry. Zoe had first seen signs pointing to the trail when she'd visited Sinksville for their annual Ramp Festival and Craft Show.

She had wangled her way onto the search team setting out to look for Susan and her estranged husband, Patrick Rourke. Her story for Ethan, which he had accepted at face value, knowing there was more to it, was that she was a neighbor and, therefore, felt obligated. But what she really felt was guilt and responsibility. Of all people, she knew very well that when an abused woman leaves her husband, he is more apt than ever to kill her.

She had not slept well the night before, and when she did manage to leave conscious thought behind, her mind juggled images of Karen. She had envisioned Karen as she had been when they had shared an apartment, Karen at her wedding to Paul, Karen laughing and then, abruptly, collapsing in midsyllable. Zoe still berated herself for that last time, still felt that if only she'd been smarter or quicker, she could've stopped Paul before he killed Karen. Each time she revisited the memory, she still found herself lacking.

She had guessed that Susan Rourke was on the run from her husband. This time even ignorance was not an excuse. She had known graphically well what could happen. But she had offered no more than lip service to Susan when she had been handed a real opportunity to do more. She felt she had no choice but to join the search. It was time to start doing. Her hope was that it was not too late.

Because it spanned two counties, the search was being coordinated by the state police. Patrick Rourke had grown up in Feller County, right next door to Bickle County. He and Susan had set up housekeeping there in Burnt Chimney after their marriage. During the Rourkes' residence, the police had answered five domestic disturbance calls. Susan had pressed charges only once and dropped them before the hearing.

They had moved to Sinksville eight months ago. There were reports of two calls to the police during their first four months in

Sinksville. Each time, no further action was taken. For the last four months, there had been an ominous quiet.

Sinksville had been home to Susan Rourke before her marriage. She had been raised a Taylor there on the land her family had owned since the area had first been settled. She had married Patrick after meeting him at the local VFW dances while she was still in high school. He had dropped out of high school during his senior year and gone to work loading, then driving, coal trucks. It was still all he knew how to do, aside from his skills in the forest, and those appeared to be finely honed.

It was common knowledge that Patrick Rourke was very familiar with the state forest land that included sections of Feller and Bickle counties and backed up into the foothills of the Allegheny Mountains. It was a dense, wild area, and if he had Susan somewhere in there, it might be quite a while before they were found. Although he had apparently used his pickup truck to get where he was going, he would not rely on it in the forest. Finding it would be only a beginning.

It was barely dawn, with colors still tending toward monochromatic, when Zoe found the state police headquartered in the parking lot at the Sinksville Ordinary, a motel, grocery store, and lunch counter all rolled into one long succession of small buildings.

The morning was cool, and there was a scent of rain in the air. The main street was damp, although a constant breeze trundled by, wheezing now and then. In spite of the sour-tasting nature of the task, Zoe's senses felt keenly edged and buzzing. The day had a kind of crisp promise to it, as if sometimes life could indeed hand out second chances.

She joined the other volunteers to get her assignment. They bunched together and drifted apart. What first seemed chaos coalesced into order as she filtered through the crowd.

As she neared the assignment officer, she watched a troop of Boy Scouts sprint out toward a spot behind the Ordinary.

A woman beside her followed her gaze. Taller than Zoe by at least a couple of inches, and more slightly built, she hinted at a smile. In a low voice she said, "Looks like a group visit to the outhouse, doesn't it?"

Zoe nodded absently, but her eyes kept scanning the hills. "Isn't that where the Pioneer Trail is?"

"That would be the Trail, all right. How did you happen to get involved in this thing? Do you know Susan or Patrick Rourke?"

Zoe looked at her with more than the cursory exam she'd given her a minute ago. "Are you a reporter?"

The woman's eyes widened, and a trace of a dimple dented her cheek. "What makes you ask that?"

It was experience whispering in her ear. "Are you?" she repeated.

Zoe's sudden coolness made the woman back up a step. "I'm a stringer for the Morgantown and Charleston papers. And I also work for the *Russell Creek Bulletin*." She said it with a lift of her chin, defiantly.

In spite of herself, Zoe smiled. She had felt besieged by reporters in D.C. after Karen and Paul died and had determined then never to let herself be cornered by them, never to see her name in the paper again. She had almost forgotten that circumstances were different in a small town.

The *Russell Creek Bulletin* was the only local paper. Published three times a week, it mostly carried stories about who was in the hospital and who was expecting visitors from out of town. In addition, every once in a while it actually covered hard news.

"I subscribe to the *Bulletin*," Zoe offered by way of appeasement. "It's a good paper."

The woman held out her mocha-colored hand. "I'm Willa Fiore."

"Zoe Kergulin."

"I guess you could tell me exactly what the Pioneer Trail is," Zoe said, her eyes following the Boy Scouts, her tone noticeably warmer. "I only know it from seeing it on the highway map."

"It's that historical pathway the state put together in the last few years. They try to promote the idea that the route follows the Underground Railroad, and there's even a marker over in front of the Ordinary that this place was a stop on the Railroad."

Her tone prompted Zoe to ask, "It wasn't?"

"It's a pity people don't learn history in school anymore, don't you think? The Underground Railroad is a myth."

Zoe did not know Willa Fiore well enough to decide whether she was kidding or not. "A myth?"

Willa shook her head as if it should have been common knowledge. "A myth. Hooey. It's like all those stories nowadays about people who saved the Jews during the Holocaust. If there were really so many heroes, why did so many Jews die? Why were so many betrayed by friends and neighbors? People are people. Self-interest tends to rule. We like to entertain highfaluting ideas about how wonderful we are, but nine times out of ten, we let people suffer rather than risk our own necks. There was no organization that helped slaves escape to freedom. There were a few individuals who helped slaves along the way north, but no concerted efforts. Slaves were mostly on their own. The idea that people helped them on their way, hid them, and gave them shelter in a place like the Ordinary is appealing, but it's a myth. And it takes away from the extraordinary courage of those few thousand, if that, who actually took it upon themselves to find freedom."

"You know, I've been here before, but it never occurred to me to ask why the place is called the Ordinary. The Ordinary what?"

"An ordinary was an inn in colonial times," Willa obliged. "The original building here is at least two hundred years old. Well, the logs are, anyway. And maybe the two sisters who run the place."

The officer in charge motioned the two women forward. Zoe and Willa were assigned to cover an area not far from where Susan Rourke had grown up. Altogether, there were six in the group, including one off-duty officer, who would act as group leader, and one search-and-rescue team member and her dog. The other two were coal truck drivers, coworkers of Patrick Rourke's. Each group was supplied with a much-photocopied topographical map, with their specific search area marked. The group leader carried the only walkie-talkie. Zoe did not see a weapon, but she would have bet that the leader was armed as well.

Technically, they were not there to find Patrick Rourke. The assignment was to determine if Susan Rourke had been kidnapped and left somewhere among the trees. The unvoiced fear they all shared was that one of them would stumble upon her body. None spoke of facing down Patrick Rourke, a man sure to be carrying at least part of his arsenal, a man who hunted and trapped year 'round, in season or not, a man who knew the woods better than many knew the towns they lived in. A man the police knew as a batterer, a man who might very well now be a murderer.

They were instructed to stay within sight of one another. No one was to touch anything that did not seem to belong where it was found, including even rocks and branches. They would be covering rough, wet terrain, searching it as thoroughly as possible.

Drizzle turned to steady rain as they walked to off-duty officer Alice Loomis's Suburban, introducing themselves as they piled inside. Wyatt Harrison, the largest of the group, burly and wide, settled into the front seat.

Phoenix, the black Labrador, belonged to Margaret Connor, a lanky woman of about thirty-five, red-haired, her pale skin dotted with freckles. Margaret coaxed the dog into the rearmost compartment and then joined him there. Willa and Zoe squeezed to the left in the backseat to make room for Sam Bennett, the other coal truck driver. Tall and wiry, his energy seemed to take up more space than he did.

As the vehicle pulled away from Sinksville, Sam leaned forward and whispered loudly, "'Member goin' for wild boars down in that hollow last year with Patrick, Wyatt? I don't think I've ever been drunker in my life!"

At the same time, Margaret was saying, "Phoenix and I got the last room at that motel. They didn't want to take us, but I think I convinced them that a well-trained dog is going to be a lot less trouble than most of their guests. Phoenix doesn't drink or smoke or steal towels. Are you all staying at the Ordinary?"

Willa shook her head but said, "It's an interesting place, isn't it?"

Margaret nodded. "And so old! You can actually touch history there."

"How do you know?" Zoe pressed Willa suddenly, having been mulling over what she had told her. "How do you know it couldn't have been a legitimate stop on the Railroad?"

"Oh, come on!" Willa answered. "They find a cellar that was probably used to hide liquor during Prohibition, and they call it a secret stop on the Underground Railroad."

The car pulled off the asphalt and started to bump along a rutted lane.

Alice Loomis's blond ponytail swung to the side as she spoke over her shoulder into the backseat. "My great-great-great-grand-father was an abolitionist from Philadelphia. He knew Levi Cotton. They worked on the Underground Railroad together."

Willa frowned. "He might have been an abolitionist, and maybe he helped people along the way, and maybe he even worked with Coffin," she corrected the name gently, "but chances were he didn't help any slaves escape their overseers. The Railroad was a figment of slaveholders' imaginations and a way to paint abolitionists as people to be scared of. Propaganda."

"Reporters are so cynical," Alice Loomis observed.

"Cynical, hell," Willa replied. "Reporters only write what the public wants nowadays. It's all human interest. When one of you guys sprains an ankle or gets poison ivy, that will make a story. Digging for the truth is a fossil itself these days."

From the rear of the car, her arms going around her dog, Margaret said sadly, "The news is that another woman is missing, and her husband has a history of beating up on her. It doesn't bode well for either one of them, does it?"

Willa shook her head. "You want to know something? No paper's interested if he beats her up. I could never sell that story to anyone. No one wants to read about that. Now if he kills her, that's a story, although everyone who reads it blames her for staying with him. If she beats him up, that's a story, and everyone thinks he must be emasculated. Don't blame reporters for that."

Sam Bennett shifted uncomfortably beside Willa, rubbing at his shoulder and frowning. She shot him a look of pity mixed with derision. "Don't tell me you're going to defend the guy?"

Wyatt turned in his seat. "If he won't, I will. Patrick Rourke hasn't been convicted yet. He's entitled to a trial, no matter what you think. And even if he did beat her up now and then, maybe she deserved it. It doesn't mean he's a lousy SOB in everything he does."

"Yes, it does," Willa said, softly but fiercely. "I don't care if he's got the humanitarian of the year award from the Grand Poobahs Association, if he beats his wife, he's a lousy SOB."

The vehicle slammed to a stop at a watery place in the muddy road. A puddle spanned the lane, and from the driver's seat, it was impossible to tell if the water was a few inches deep or a few feet.

Alice maneuvered far to the side and shut off the engine as she announced, "Okay! This is as good a place as any. There's a fire road just ahead that leads up to a parking area below the Taylor house. That's where Susan Rourke grew up. Someone's up there with her sister now. So far, there's been no sign of Susan, but we're going on the assumption that she may try to get home. We're going to explore this mountain, from bottom to top, just to let Susan know, if she's around, that it's safe to come out. We'll start with the road. I'll take the right side. Margaret, you and your dog take the left. The rest of you fan out, two on my side, two on Margaret's. Whatever you do, don't lose sight of the person on either side of you. The last thing we need is to have to come in here after one of you."

Zoe donned the lightweight day pack she had brought, slipped her poncho over her head, and pulled on a hat. The rain was falling at a day-eating pace now, heavy and steady. Her canvas shoes, sturdy and waterproofed, were already soaked through.

As if a signal had been prearranged, Alice nodded, and they fanned out, the two men on Margaret's side, while Willa and Zoe took the right. They stayed close enough so that they were not likely to miss anything between them as they made their slow climb up the mountain.

Fog lay like guerrillas in trenches, waiting in ambush in depressions no deeper than a fallen tree. The searchers' breathing mingled with it and then dispersed, leaving only the lurking mist behind.

Zoe had not brought gloves, and her fingers were recalcitrant with the cold. She pulled the damp sleeves of the sweater over her hands and kept on going.

No one said much, their minds occupied with the search. Phoenix gave a happy grunt now and then, but he made no huzzas of discovery.

After more than two hours of nose-down plodding, they reached the parking area below the Taylor house. It was graded and graveled, and big enough for three or four cars to park and exit without too much jockeying. A rusting red pickup was parked pulled off to one side, and a blue Saturn, no more than a couple of years old, sat nearby.

The party crowded into a three-sided shed set off to one side against the mountain. A snowplow rested against the back wall, along with two shovels and a couple of broken ice scrapers. A small pile of sawdust was slowly returning to earth in one back corner, and the cemented dregs of a road salt cache sat in the other.

Although they had been out only a couple of hours, everyone was wet and tired, as if the rainwater had percolated energy from them. The dread anticipation of finding a body, coupled with the constant, ever-thwarted hope that their group would be the one to find Susan Rourke alive, proved to be emotionally wearing. Slipping on wet leaves and the underlying rocks added to the physical toll.

Alice Loomis passed around a plastic bag of raisins and peanuts, and their pale faces huddled close, silently eating. Four deer poked their heads through the veil of fog at the edge of the parking area. The searchers all nudged each other and watched the animals evaluate the degree of threat before they slipped back over the ridge and out of sight.

Alice sighed. "I wish it were hunting season right now."

"Yeah," Sam and Wyatt agreed.

Willa's jaw hardened. "When you see a majestic sunset, do you want to shoot that, too?"

"Shh," Margaret intoned. "I hear something."

They all quieted. The sound came again, a faint cry, as if a baby had been buried under mounds of blankets.

"I don't hear anything," Sam whispered, although Phoenix was straining toward the sound.

Alice's walkie-talkie crackled, and everyone jumped. Zoe heard only garbled static, even when Alice asked the sender to repeat the message. But the trooper somehow unscrambled it.

"They found Patrick Rourke's truck west of here," she said, pulling out her map. "About four miles as the crow flies. About four hours or more if we try it on foot. Let's head back to the truck and drive over. They're concentrating the search there."

Everyone began groaning and stretching.

"Wait!" Margaret insisted. "Phoenix and I heard something down that hillside."

Alice shook her head. "It's not part of this search."

"What if it's Susan Rourke, lying hurt out there?"

Alice simultaneously turned her head, rolled her eyes, and sighed loudly. But she resolutely picked up the radio and called in, informing the search leaders that her group was going to check out a sound they had heard. She assured them it wouldn't take long. As soon as she signed off, she stared at Margaret.

In turn, Margaret looked at the dog, and they were off. She and Phoenix took the lead, with Zoe a close second. Someone needed rescuing. With luck, maybe it would be Susan Rourke.

Phoenix leaped happily through the wet undergrowth, his nostrils flaring to capture every bit of the scent he followed. Every so often he turned to look at Margaret, smiling that doggy grin that revealed how deliriously grateful he was to be tramping through muck and cold on a rainy fall day with the person he loved best in the world.

They ran downhill, branches swiping at clothes and faces, scattered raindrops arcing out behind after they had passed. Zoe skidded into a sapling, apologized without thinking, and kept on going.

After a brief sprint, the dog slowed, and so did they.

"Hold onto him," Zoe told Margaret unnecessarily, for the woman was already instructing the dog to sit and stay.

In front of them towered a tall hemlock. There were not many left around the area, but this one looked to be virgin growth. Beside it crouched a stunted maple, rooted in perpetual shade. And under the maple lay a bedraggled orange cat, his mouth open to make one more pitiful cry, his front paw stretched out perpendicular to his side, a huge steel-jawed leghold trap pinching off circulation.

"Careful!" Margaret cautioned. "Sometimes they bite. And there've been reports of rabid cats around here."

Zoe went forward anyway. She knew cats, had felt an affinity with them all her life. She had left them behind when she moved to D.C., but now they lived with her again. Zoe flinched upon closer examination of this cat. His paw was swollen to cartoon size. Blood spattered his tabby coat. Orange eyes widened at her approach, and he opened his mouth again, but no sound came out.

Ducking out of her poncho, Zoe slipped off the day pack. The rain sent icy fingers down her neck, sliding under her sweater, soaking into her shirt.

Wyatt slid to a halt beside her and, in a low voice, offered, "I'll find a stick or a rock and put him out of his misery." Looking back toward Sam, he added, "Too bad you didn't have those hounds of yours here. They'd have taken care of things."

"Let's give him a chance first." Zoe looked down at her sweater. It was not thick enough to protect her hands in case the cat bit in fear or pain.

Alice slid to a stop and wiped her forehead, leaving behind a muddy streak. She shook her head. "We've got to meet up with the others. There's no time to deal with a feral cat who's likely to die soon anyway."

"He's not going to die!" Zoe said fiercely as she dumped the contents of her day pack onto the wet poncho. An apple, a canteen, a paperback book, a clean pair of socks, an emergency space blanket, and a cheap pair of binoculars cascaded down. She didn't really need any of it but was glad she had brought the pack.

Approaching the cat cautiously, she softly whispered nonsense. With a quick lunge, she managed to grab him by the scruff. His back legs shifted, but he made no other move.

"I need some help getting him into this pack." She looked up, ready to pick a volunteer, but Willa immediately stepped forward. "Let's try not to jostle his paw."

With great care, they eased him backward into the pack until only his paw and the attached trap stuck out.

Wyatt and Sam released the trap while Zoe kept hold of the orange cat, who gave a mighty yowl. He struggled now, but had nowhere to go.

She stood up with her bundle, tugging the zipper closed, while Willa gathered up those things she had carried.

"It would've been easier just to kill him," Wyatt muttered.

"Is it one of Patrick Rourke's traps?" Zoe asked, hugging the pack close to her middle, hunching over it to protect the soaked cat from the rain.

Sam nodded, but Wyatt said, "Who knows?"

"There's no vet in Sinksville," Margaret announced bleakly. "It might be easier to let the little guy go, let nature take its course."

"We do have to get to the area where the truck was found," Alice added with a glance at her watch. "We can't waste time looking for a vet."

"I'll find help for him without holding you back." Zoe pointed with her chin, her hands being otherwise occupied. "Isn't the fire road we came up over that way?"

The only thing she could think of was to get him to her own vet as quickly as possible. That meant dropping out of the search, at least temporarily, and driving him back to Russell Creek, where her veterinarian was headquartered. She did not want to leave, not when there was still a chance to find Susan Rourke alive, not when every minute might be the difference between life and death. But Zoe had accepted responsibility for the injured cat the instant she saw him in the trap, and her immediate task was seeing to his needs.

As they headed back toward Sinksville in Alice's car, the cat was passive in the bag in Zoe's lap. He weighed no more than a hearty loaf of bread. Zoe had no idea how long he had been there. For the cat's sake, she hoped it had not been as long as a few days. In fear of either letting him loose in the car or finding him dead, she did not unzip the pack.

Her thoughts inevitably strayed to Susan Rourke. Was she somewhere out there, similarly trapped? Held hostage not by steel, but by a crazed and desperate man?

No one spoke much on the ride back, although Alice's radio crackled steadily. Reports of sighting a man with a gun fizzled into the presence of another search team in the area, one of its members carrying a walking stick. Another team radioed in that a sock had been found, but it was moldy and eaten through, and not likely to belong to Susan or Patrick Rourke.

Each report had everyone straining forward to distinguish the words, only tensing more when the initial discovery proved illusory.

Alice kindly dropped Zoe at her car. Before Zoe got out with her now limp bundle, Alice turned around in the seat and showed her the map. She circled a small area where Zoe could meet up with them again, provided she got back before the search was called for the day. As Zoe climbed out, cradling the pack against her stomach, Willa deposited the rest of her gear on the floor of the front seat of her car. Until that moment, Zoe had not realized that the leghold trap had made the trip down the mountainside along with everything else. Now it was in her car.

Willa had barely gotten back inside Alice's vehicle before it made a tight U-turn and headed back toward the search area.

Zoe watched them leave with a tightness in her chest and a wish for Susan Rourke's safe return on her lips. She hurried her own trip, stopping at the vet's in Russell Creek only long enough for the staff there to reassure her that the cat would likely survive, although his leg might not.

She carried the empty, soiled pack back to her car, having no desire to put anything back inside it. Instead, she threw it onto the floor on top of the other debris and headed back to Sinksville.

The police at the Ordinary were able to show her exactly where she could locate her team. Back in the car, she drove down yet another fire road—this one in slightly worse shape than the one earlier—and, after a mile of following tire tracks pressed in mud, parked behind Alice's Suburban. From there, an arrow made of twigs pointed her into the woods.

Where there was grass, it was flattened by the passage of feet. Where the ground was bare, she followed either footprints in muck or more arrows.

Rain still pattered around her, seeming almost a drizzle under some trees and, when the wind blew, a huge torrent under others.

One arrow pointed across a swollen stream. The water moved swiftly, perhaps at a deeper level than when her team had forded it some time earlier. In deference to wet feet and icy toes, she scouted around for another place to cross.

Just around a couple of bends, maybe eighty yards farther, the stream widened, and the tops of huge rocks poked above the current. That looked to her like a safer, drier bet. Relying on momentum more than planning, Zoe leapt from wet surface to wet surface until, with a final surge, she landed safely on the opposite bank.

Once there, though, she was unsure of the exact direction to take. The grayness of the day, the inability to see the sky, robbed her of her sense of direction. She knew she had to head downstream to pick up the designated path again, but a thicket of brambles prevented her from doing so right away. Keeping the stream at her back, she set out, with the intention of taking a sharp left as soon as the bushes allowed. As long as she kept within hearing distance of the stream, she knew she would not stray too far from her immediate destination.

Ahead of her, she spotted someone pacing stiffly back and forth between two trees. She almost called out, thinking it must be a member of her own team, even though this man was short, built unlike either Sam or Wyatt. As Zoe drew nearer, she saw that the man's lips were chapped, his jacket soaked, and his thin hair wet and pasted to his skull.

As soon as he became aware of Zoe, he froze. His hand rose. "Stay back!" he ordered. "Don't come any closer!"

"What's the matter? Are you okay?" Zoe's eyes searched the surrounding bushes for a clue to what might be wrong.

"My team, we found the body. No one's supposed to go near it until the police get here. The upper part's just about blown away. Shotgun blast. Not something you want to think about, believe me."

"Oh," Zoe said, feeling her center of gravity shift downwards. She was too late. "Any sign of Patrick Rourke?" She heard her professional voice take over the questioning.

The man's mouth twisted wryly. "Any sign of Susan Rourke, you mean. It's Patrick's body we found!"

Zoe fought her way out from under a blanket of wet leaves and cats that had somehow become entangled in her dreams. After a couple of fruitless gropes, she grabbed the phone, her heart hammering. "Hello?"

"Hey, Zo," Ethan said apologetically. "I know you were up late, but I thought you'd want to know."

She sat up, reaching for a pen and paper, hugging the phone between shoulder and ear.

"They found her?" The various teams had spent well into the night searching for Susan Rourke, calling her name, beating through the dripping vegetation. Maybe Patrick Rourke had killed his estranged wife elsewhere, then turned the weapon on himself. No trace of Susan had been found.

"We want to talk to her in connection with Patrick Rourke's murder. There's a stop out on her." He meant that a warrant had been issued.

"What? It wasn't suicide?"

"The medical examiner is estimating the shotgun was fired from four to six feet away."

The professional part of Zoe's brain quickly clicked on, neurons fairly humming. "Was he shot where he was found?"

"Preliminary findings say no. And there was nothing in the tree behind the body, so that supports the hypothesis. But the exact spot where he was shot hasn't been determined yet. She may not have dragged him far—I doubt if she *could* have dragged him far—but the weather didn't exactly cooperate in the search. The rain probably took care of a lot of the evidence. It looks as if she took her opportunity, grabbed the shotgun, and let him have it."

"But it makes no sense. Why move the body?"

"Hey, I only have the questions, too, not the answers."

Zoe rubbed at an eye with the knuckles of the hand holding the pen. "Has it been determined that Susan Rourke's fingerprints are on the murder weapon?"

In her mind's eye, she could see Ethan settle back in his desk chair. She glanced at the bedside alarm clock and wondered how long he had already been at work that morning. It was barely seven.

He said, "I haven't heard anything on that yet. The crime lab will be working on it, though." He meant the State Police Crime Lab in Charleston.

"Why Susan, though? Even in the throes of an adrenaline rush, how far could she move him?"

"Zo, she's the one he allegedly kidnapped. She has years of abuse as the motive. At least that's been documented somewhat. She certainly had the means, and out in the woods alone with the guy, she couldn't have had a better opportunity."

Zoe did not want Susan Rourke to be guilty. She knew what it was to kill an abuser, and the thought of Susan having to go through the gauntlet that occurred when the tables were turned put a sour taste in her mouth.

Not that Zoe felt sorry for Patrick Rourke. She knew she should have mustered up some empathic feeling for him, but she found herself unable to dredge up anything more than regret for a wasted life. She was not sorry that a man unable to control his violent impulses could no longer take them out on the one person least likely to resist them. At least Susan would be safe from him now. Alive or dead, Zoe thought gloomily.

"Do you have any idea where she might be?" she asked.

"A team's going back to the trailer behind your house this morning. Maybe there's a clue that's been overlooked. My guess is she's still in the woods somewhere. If she's alive, she'll probably try to contact her sister, in that house near where you were yesterday. Susan's got no car. There's a watch out on the use of her credit cards. She can't get far. She'll turn up soon."

"Unless he killed her first." Zoe was thinking of Karen, of Paul Martin lying in wait, of her friend dropping dead beside her. Ethan knew it.

She could hear in his voice how he tried to find something to smile about. "That would be a nifty trick: him killing her and then her killing him."

"Stranger things have happened in these West Virginia hills. Ethan, can the time of death be estimated yet?"

"The preliminary report says early morning yesterday. Maybe even late the night before. That's as definite as things are so far."

"Can you get me a list of things that were found in Patrick Rourke's truck?"

"Why? What are you looking for? No one's hired you, Zoe."

She had been installing security systems and protocols for that very reason. "Not yet, Ethan. But the attorney Susan Rourke hires is going to need a good private investigator to support her case. I might as well have the information handy." She paused. Lying, or at least not telling the complete truth, was not where she wanted to end the conversation. Ethan deserved better. "I feel as if I've failed again, Ethan. I couldn't protect Karen, and I didn't even offer to help Susan. I let her down once. I don't want to do it again."

He sighed. "Karen's death wasn't your fault, and you know it. Paul Martin would have killed her whenever he got the opportunity."

"Can you get me that list?" she asked.

He sighed again. "I'll see what I can do."

On her way to Sinksville, Zoe stopped first in Russell Creek to see the cat she already considered her new fellow. She didn't have a name for him yet, although she tried out some potential candidates on the drive over. Nothing seemed to fit yet. He was registered in the hospital as "Stray Kergulin."

The small-animal veterinarian, Jill Simone, a skillful practitioner Zoe had come to think of as a friend as well as a dependent she could not claim on her tax form, took Zoe into the back, where the cages stood like the palace guard against the wall. The green tiled floor was spotless, and the air smelled strongly of disinfectant.

"So?" Zoe prompted.

"Well, he's very run down. Dehydrated, too. That's not surprising." She tucked her long brown hair behind her ears. "We're trying to build him up right now; otherwise, he won't survive the surgery. It still looks pretty definite that he's going to lose that front leg. That situation may change, but I wouldn't bet on it. Whichever way it goes, he's also going to have to be neutered, of course. And vaccinated. And we'll test him for feline leukemia and a few other things. The leg's the main concern for the moment."

"How long would you say he was in that trap?"

"Way over the limit. Three or four days at the very least. It could even be longer. Someone should have been checking his traps. There was no reason for this cat to suffer there for so long."

While Jill got back to her clients, Zoe communed with the new boy. He was in no mood for lovemaking, but neither would she be, she thought, were their places reversed. At least she knew he was safe and in good hands. The rest could wait until later.

The day had begun overcast, but as Zoe drove to Sinksville, the sun burst through like a flower in time-lapse photography, spilling its light across the craggy land. She rolled down the window a bit and reveled in the cool, invigorating air. This was her time of the year: sweater weather, crisp breezes, changeable skies.

About two miles outside of Sinksville, she saw a blue Saturn up ahead, pulled off to the side of the road. She recognized the car. Only the day before, it had been parked in the lot where her team had taken a break, where Margaret Connor and her dog had heard the cat crying. Zoe braked and studied the young woman, who was wearing a suit that was a size or two too small for her, as she, in turn, stood frowning at the driver's door.

Zoe pulled off the road and came to a stop just behind the blue car.

"Can I help? Give you a lift?" she offered.

The woman was in her midtwenties, her fashionably styled hair cut to chin length, thick and slightly curled under on the ends. It was blond and shiny, and parted in the middle. When she looked down, it swung forward and covered her face. It appeared that she spent a lot of time looking down. Zoe followed the other woman's gaze to her shoes, which were flat and sturdy.

Glancing up without raising her chin, the woman said, more to the ground than to Zoe, "He bought me the damn cheap tires. I said I wanted the good ones, but he thinks he knows best. He thinks he's getting me a deal!" She shook her head. "I got a damn flat!"

"I'll help you change it."

"I'd change it myself if I had a spare! But, damn him! He takes the spare out, says he's got some hauling to do, says he'll put it back when he's done, and now I look and guess what? No spare! Damn fool probably lost it!"

"Well, at least let me give you a ride into town. You can call someone for help."

"Who'm I going to call? Him?"

"I could give you a lift to a service station in Sinksville. Maybe they can patch the tire for you."

Grudgingly, the other woman said, "Yeah, okay. I guess that would work." Belatedly, she added, "Thanks. I do appreciate it. Let me get out of this getup first, though. Okay?"

Zoe shrugged. "Sure."

Ludicrous as it seemed on a main road, Zoe wanted to give the woman some privacy, so she busied herself in the trunk of her car, taking her time pulling out the jack and the lug wrench. Compared to the jumble in the backseat of the car, the trunk was relatively pristine.

Even though it was the major artery into Sinksville, not a single vehicle passed. Zoe kept an eye out for traffic as she fiddled around under cover of the trunk lid, mostly reseating her own spare tire. Eventually the young woman joined her, head cocked as if she could not fathom what had been going on inside that trunk.

"I've got some stuff we might need," Zoe announced, scanning the flares and equipment she had gathered. "Everything except a spare tire that would fit your car, anyway."

"I wondered what you were doing under there."

The young woman had changed into baggy jeans and a loose plaid flannel shirt. The shoes were the same, but socks had been added. These clothes fit her, both in size and, seemingly, in temperament. She was more relaxed, surer of her movements.

They removed the flat with little difficulty. After slinging the thing into the trunk, Zoe slammed the lid and went to the passenger side to unlock that door. Until that moment, she had forgotten about the mess on the floor.

"Hold on a sec and I'll clean this out for you," she said, tossing articles into the general mayhem that was a constant in the backseat. Under her day pack and the paperback book, she found the leghold trap. It caught her attention for a moment, bringing back the events of the day before, and then she poised to heave it over the seat.

A hand on her arm stopped the motion. "Wait. Where'd you get that?"

"It was attached to a cat I found yesterday. Is it yours?"

"No way! It's Patrick's. Well, it was Patrick's."

"Are you sure?"

She nodded and then pointed to a metal tag. "It's got his phone number right there."

"You were a friend of Patrick Rourke's?" Zoe figured she already knew who the young woman was, but she had learned not to rely on leaping to conclusions until she could measure the length of the jump.

The other woman pursed her lips. "Well, I wouldn't exactly say a friend. I was related to him, kind of. He was married to my sister."

"You're —" Zoe knew the last name was Taylor, but she realized she had not heard the woman's first name. She completed her sentence with, "Susan's sister."

Holding out her hand, the younger woman smiled. "Laurel Taylor."

"Zoe Kergulin."

As they shook hands, Laurel's hair swept forward and hid her face. "Do you know Susan?"

"Not really. I met her after she moved into the trailer on the property next door to mine. We talked a couple of times. I was hoping to get to know her better."

Laurel's eyes returned to the ground. "Yeah."

"Have you had any word?"

"Nope. The police say it's too soon to give up hope, and I certainly haven't."

"I was helping to look for her yesterday. Is there anyplace you can think of where she might run for help?" Zoe watched Laurel take a step away from her and close up, like a vault door on a time lock. She knew Laurel Taylor had heard a lot of the same questions lately.

She hastened to explain, "I'm a private investigator, Laurel. I'm not a reporter, and I'm not with the police. Your sister didn't hire me and neither did anyone else, but I want to help her. I want to find out whatever I can that will help in her defense."

Laurel raised her chin. Her gray eyes were flat, her words clipped. "He only tried to kill her about a bazillion times. Other than that, I guess she doesn't have any defense at all."

"Sometimes that's not enough," Zoe said softly.

She was thinking, as always, of Karen, who had pressed charges against Paul more than once. But no one, including Karen, wanted to believe that an outstanding employee of the Justice Department would abuse his own wife.

Zoe leaned against the car. "Where do you think she is?"

Laurel shrugged.

"I know the police must have asked you, too, Laurel, and the last thing I want to do is push you or rub salt in a wound, but surely you've been thinking of where she might have gone."

Laurel raised her chin a bit, and her eyes defiantly met Zoe's from under a still-lowered brow. "She used to come home. To where I live, I mean."

"But she stopped?"

"After she moved back to Sinksville. It was too close, I guess. Patrick came over a couple of times and broke some stuff. After that, whenever I saw him coming, I'd just lock myself and the dogs in the house and show him my gun. He was wild when he was after her. You wouldn't want to mess with him. No one would."

They slipped inside the car and fastened their seatbelts. Zoe started the engine and pulled out onto the empty road.

Suddenly Laurel cocked her chin at her. "Hey, are you the one with that big house in the woods?"

"The Queen Anne? Yeah, that would be mine."

Laurel brightened and warmed. "I snuck over to Beverage to see Susan last week. She took me down to show me that place, but you weren't home. If you can afford a house like that, what are you doing driving an old heap like this?"

Zoe laughed. "I bought the house five years ago. I was working in D.C. then, and I had a pretty good income." Her savings as well as her retirement had gone much further in Bickle County than money ever had in Alexandria, Virginia.

"When I saw that place," Zoe continued, "it was love at first sight. It hadn't been occupied for over three years, and it wasn't in the best of shape. It still isn't. I just can't afford to keep it in the manner to which it should be accustomed."

"I thought you built it yourself." Laurel was a little disappointed.

Zoe smiled and shook her head. Whatever its shape, in her mind she saw the house in its full glory, as it was meant to be. "No. It was built over a hundred years ago, for a coal mine owner and his new French bride. An architect from Boston designed it."

She liked to think that her great-great-grandmother, one of

the first female organizers to come to coal country, would have liked the idea of a coal miner's kid living in the owner's house. It was the kind of tables-turned comeuppance her family used to glorify.

Laurel shook her head. "Wow! My great-granddad built our house. We kind of added on to it over the years, but it doesn't look anything like your house. All those little nooks and doodads everywhere! And it all fits together so nice! Do you think someone cut all that lacy woodwork by hand?"

Zoe warned herself not to get started. She knew from experience that not everyone had an affinity for window seats, sunlight through stained glass, towers, turrets, and so many built-in, custom-made niceties that she was still discovering them. While she would be raptly detailing yet another unique feature of the place, others' eyes would begin to glaze over.

So she settled for, "Yeah, I do. You're welcome to come see the inside sometime, if you'd like."

"Cool! Thanks!"

Her eyes on the road, the smile slowly fading from her face, Zoe abruptly sobered. "Laurel, when you went to visit your sister, was there any way you could have been followed?"

"Don't you think I've already asked myself that? But I kept my eyes on the rearview mirror the whole time! And I didn't even use my own car! He didn't follow me! I'm sure of it."

She said it with so much conviction that Zoe knew Laurel had to be still questioning herself, going back over the details of that ride across the county, wondering if there had been some way Patrick Rourke had managed to follow her without being seen himself.

"Do you have any other sisters or brothers, besides Susan?" she asked, deliberately changing the subject.

Laurel shook her head, and once again her hair shielded her from outside view. "I had an older brother. Tucker, his name was.

But he and my mom drowned over in Triple Lake one year. He was twelve, and I don't really remember him much anymore. I was only eight when he died. Susan, though, she was already fourteen. She had wanted to go along, but it was her time of the month, and Mama wouldn't let her."

For a brief instant, Zoe took her eyes from the road. Laurel raised her head to meet Zoe's glance, and she did not look away when Zoe's immediate attention returned to her driving.

"Were you there?" Zoe asked, not deliberately whispering, although that was how it came out. Laurel's recitation had been emotionless, the way Zoe's tended to be when she talked about Karen. It did not at all mean that feelings were not churning, down deep.

"No. I wasn't old enough, they said. Susan and I stayed with Aunt Ardell and Aunt Ruth over at the Ordinary. They're not really our aunts, but they looked out for us after that, when they could."

"That must have been a terrible time for you, losing your brother and mother like that."

Laurel nodded. "He was the prize of the family, that's for sure. Mama and Daddy put all their hopes on his shoulders. And he was so handsome! Daddy never forgave himself, or Tucker, neither, I think. Daddy almost drowned back then, too, jumping in after Mama and Tuck. But the people who hit our boat managed to pull him out. After that, Daddy started drinking again."

Zoe decelerated and pulled into the gas station just as Laurel added, "Sometimes I think Susan and I would have been a lot better off if those people had just left Daddy in the water."

It was afternoon by the time Zoe pulled into the parking lot at the Ordinary. She had helped Laurel get the repaired tire back on the car, then watched as the younger woman headed toward home. When the flat occurred, Laurel had been on her way back from Patrick Rourke's parents' house, where she had gone in order to pay her respects. It had not taken her long.

She told Zoe she was planning on spending the rest of the day with "him," the man who had bought the cheap tires, the one she wouldn't name. The two women arranged to meet the following day. Laurel said she thought she knew where Patrick had kept his traps, and Zoe wanted to make sure all were empty and disabled. Fairly certain that detail was far from the agenda of the state police investigation, she hoped it would give her an opportunity to talk further with Laurel and to find out where she and Susan used to spend their time as children. It was a long shot, given that there were six years between the sisters, but it was still a possibility.

Meanwhile, Zoe stepped out of her car into an almost-empty expanse. The army that had been mobilized for the search only the day before had moved on, and the parking lot ran flat as a calm sea to an overgrown meadow and a fleet of buildings, beginning with the largest. The sign on the outside read, "Sinksville Ordinary. Supplies and Facilities."

That sign in no way prepared her for the leap into the past a step inside brought. Huge logs defined the walls. Outside, insulation and siding had been added, but inside, ancient, dark timber held sway. Trees of that circumference no longer grew in any forest in the world.

The Ordinary was dark inside, with a diffuse light provided by numerous table lamps with wide shades that threw elongated ovals of soft luminescence onto bins of potatoes, squash, and flashlight batteries. Snowshoes and homemade baskets cast weird shadows from the high ceiling where they hung. The place smelled of apples, sweets, and oil soap.

It was even larger than it appeared from the outside. The general store took up most of the space, but in the far right corner, which was obviously a much more recent addition, a large window illuminated a lunch counter, stools, and a few tables scattered haphazardly across the floor.

Zoe's eye took a quick trek around the place. At the lunch counter, someone turned in her direction. As the woman waved, Zoe recognized the slim figure of Willa Fiore, the newspaper reporter she had met the day before.

Wending her way carefully across the wide plank floor, dodging bushels of Appalachian stomper dolls, souvenir animals made of coal, and apple candy, Zoe made for the stool whose seat Willa had exaggeratedly patted.

"I didn't expect to see you so soon," Willa said, smiling, as Zoe slipped in beside her. "Are you joining the search again?"

Willa wore a shiny gray and white warm-up ensemble, which, on her, looked classy and chic. Zoe had not realized that she lacked any fashion sense until she went away to college, but she could now quickly recognize someone gifted with innate style.

Zoe's own clothes tended toward tunic sweaters over jeans or, for more formal occasions, trousers. On her, clothes simply looked comfortable. She admired Willa's style without aspiring to it.

"Has anything new turned up today?" Zoe asked.

Willa shook her head ruefully. "I wish."

A freckle-faced young man, with light brown hair cut bowl style and a cook's apron folded and tied at his waist, smiled broadly as he emerged from the kitchen, both arms lined with plates. After delivering the food to a couple of backpackers, he approached the two women.

"What can I get you folks?"

After they ordered, Zoe looked out the window, watching two old women arguing with each other as they crossed the overgrown meadow.

The sun glinted off the reddish-brown hair of the shorter of the two women. She gesticulated boisterously, making her short curls bob and weave. The other woman was taller by a bit, broader in the shoulder and hip, and wore her gray hair pulled into a loose bun fastened at the back of her head. A shawl was draped around her shoulders. Her gestures were limited to a quick movement of the head or hand.

As the young man set down two mugs of coffee on the counter, the two old women disappeared around the corner of the addition.

There was a disturbance in the kitchen, and the women emerged, both still in the throes of their discussion. The taller one made her lips a thin line as she raised her threadbare eyebrows. "You can say what you want, Ardell, but I know who it was, and so do you. You always were too stubborn to admit it when you made a mistake—"

"And you? You always have to be right, Ruth! It's been true since the day you were born. You can't see anyone else's—"

Ruth had tugged at Ardell's sweater to alert her that they were no longer alone. The two women immediately dropped their contentiousness and began greeting the customers in the diner.

Willa waved them over. "Hey, you two. I want you to meet my friend Zoe. We were on the same search team yesterday. Zoe, this is Ruth Cook, and this is her sister, Ardell Lamb."

Ruth said, "What a tragedy for that Patrick Rourke, isn't it? Our mother always said that there was no problem so huge that you had to take your life over it. Why, the solution could be right around the corner, but you'd never get there to see it."

Zoe nodded as she pressed her cold fingers against the side of the hot mug. "Actually, on the radio on the way over here, I heard there's some question as to whether or not Patrick Rourke took his own life. I'm sure we'll all hear the full report as soon as it's in."

Ruth and Ardell exchanged a glance. Ruth let her shawl fall over her arms and said, "How strange that Ardell and I were just discussing that. Tell me, Zoe, did you see anything out of the ordinary when you were up that mountain? Something that maybe raised the hair on your neck or gave you goose bumps?"

She knew what Ruth was asking, had heard plenty about haunts from neighbors when she was a child, but she shook her head in feigned ignorance. "No, nothing like that."

Ardell crowed triumphantly. "What did I tell you, Ruth? Always think you know best!"

Ruth leaned closer. "I'm talking about ghosts, Zoe. Don't tell me you didn't feel or see anything. Everyone knows that Tucker Taylor still walks these hills. He was Susan's brother, you know. He died years ago. Drowned, down in Triple Lake. I'm betting that something scary happened up on that mountain. Something sinister. I've seen that ghost! It like to give me a heart attack that time I was up there picking huckleberries one evening. I never did make that pie! You can tell us if you saw him, Zoe. We'd understand. He'd be a young man, younger than our Billy over there. But with water lilies dripping around his neck and sand in his mouth."

Ardell gently shoved her sister with her palm. "Go on, Ruth! You're going to scare off the tourists before they've even eaten."

"Did you see him, Zoe? Or feel his presence?"

"I'm sorry, Ms. Cook, but I didn't."

"You didn't walk through a wall of cold air, feel the hair rise on the back of your neck?"

Again, Zoe shook her head. "It was cold everywhere yesterday. I think my toes still haven't regained feeling. I didn't notice anyplace where it might have been colder than any other."

Ruth stood, straightened her shoulders as if she had a crick in her neck, and sighed. "Well, he still could have been there before you, you know. There's nothing that says a ghost has to hang around after he's frightened or killed someone. But what makes you say Patrick didn't kill himself?"

"It's possible, I said. That's all the radio said. I'm waiting to hear the medical examiner's report the same as you." She would no more have divulged what Ethan had told her than she would have kicked a cat, but she saw no harm in discussing what she had, indeed, heard on the radio.

"Well, I think maybe Tucker saw Patrick hurting his sister. Maybe he killed Patrick because of that." Ruth nodded up and down like a rear-window dog. "Yep, I'll bet you that's what happened. I'll bet you he killed Patrick to avenge his sister. He would be that kind, wanting to protect his own."

Ardell looked toward the ceiling, for assistance, before she said, "I apologize for my sister. She's always going around with these half-baked theories. You two would have no way of knowing Tuck Taylor if you did meet his ghost. He was a young man who drowned, oh, fifteen or so years ago."

"And he was Susan Taylor's brother!" snapped Ruth. "Let's not forget that!"

"He and Susan never got along, and you know it!" To Willa and Zoe, Ardell stage-whispered, "Too close in age."

"What do you think happened to Susan, Ms. Lamb?" Zoe asked her.

"I have no idea. And do, please, call me Ardell. And my sister here is Ruth. There's no one around who calls us by any other names. Anyway, I just hope Susan's all right. Ruth and I helped raise that girl, you know."

Billy brought their sandwiches, setting down the plates carefully, as if he had all day, despite the arrival of four more parties clamoring for service.

Sam Bennett, the wiry coal truck driver Zoe had met during the search for Susan, took a seat at the counter on the other side of Willa. She nodded to him in greeting. Beside him, his friend Wyatt Harrison settled in and nodded back.

"You two eat," Ruth urged, deliberately ignoring her sister. "We've got some inventory to take over in the Ordinary."

"Wait," Zoe said. "I'd like to talk to you about the Underground Railroad."

Ruth and Ardell exchanged a look, and Willa waved her hand as if trying to ward away cigarette smoke.

Ruth nodded toward the reporter. "Willa tells us the Underground Railroad is a myth."

"Just like bra burning," Willa nodded. "It was invented by those opposed to feminism. But how often nowadays do you hear women denounce feminism by saying, 'I'm no bra burner.' Same damn thing. The slave owners invented the Railroad."

Ruth frowned and said, "Of course the legends are true."

Right beside her, Ardell nodded and said, "The main building of this Ordinary is almost two hundred years old! These logs have seen a sight more adventure than any of us. Why, there's even a hidden cellar under the floor! You tell me what it was used for if not for helping runaway slaves!"

"Hiding liquor during Prohibition?" Willa asked innocently.

Ardell patted Zoe's hand. "Would you like to see our cellar, Zoe?"

Ruth batted ineffectually at her sister. "Oh, Ardell, no one's been down there for months! Except for those two officers. I haven't dusted, and I know you haven't, either!" She put a hand to her cheek and shook her head toward Willa and Zoe. "Two state police officers asked to take a look. One of them had toured down there as a schoolchild, and he remembered it. You see the value of involving a child in history? We used to take classes on field trips down there, and Ardell and I would tell them stories we'd heard. We'd get dressed up and everything. Then, a few years back, what with school funding cuts and the two of us getting too old to keep running up and down those rickety stairs, we stopped giving the tours and people stopped asking to have a look. I'm not sure anymore which one happened first."

"You said two officers were here to have a look down there," Zoe prompted. "Because of Susan's disappearance?"

"It surely was! Just yesterday, as a matter of fact. They were looking for clues, I suppose, although I can't imagine who would have thought that Patrick might have hidden out down there."

"Maybe they thought Susan sought refuge down there, that she'd managed to get away from Patrick and hide," Zoe suggested. "You would probably represent safety to her. And she'd know about that hiding spot."

Ardell nodded vigorously, apparently the only way she knew how. "I'll bet you that's it, Ruth! After all, Susan did practically grow up here. She knew about the cellar."

"That must be it, all right," Ruth agreed. "You should have seen those two officers, coming up from down there with dust and cobwebs all over their uniforms. If our dear mother, may she rest in peace, could have seen it! We'd've both gotten a whipping! But it's all we can do these days to keep what's open properly dusted and cleaned."

"Would you mind if I had a look in the cellar?" Zoe asked.

"Surely you don't want to go down there after what you've just heard?"

"It just makes me more curious. I'd love to see what a stop on the Underground Railroad looked like." She was also curious for the same reason the police had been. Maybe there was a place down there where a runaway wife could hide. She wasn't pinning her hopes on it, but it was a place to begin. Besides, it was a link to Susan, and at this point, she wanted any insight she might get.

"No such thing as the Underground Railroad," Willa muttered.

"Want to come with me?"

"Yeah! As a matter of fact, I do! I dare you to show me any evidence of an Underground Railroad."

Ruth gathered her shawl around her. "Well, it's cold down there, so I'd suggest you drink something warm now. You two finish eating, and Ardell and I will get started on our inventory. When you're done, you come over into the Ordinary, and we'll see how much history we can remember, between the two of us."

"Oops!" Willa slipped and missed a step.

"You okay?" Zoe asked, not daring to take her eyes from her own feet. The stairs were narrow and rickety. In the shadows cast by the flashlight, they seemed rotten and imminently ready for collapse at the next footfall.

The beam of light picked out the officers' steps in the dust. It was clear they had come to the bottom of the stairs, cast their own lights around the cellar, and then gone back up. Beyond the disturbed dust at the bottom of the stairs, filled with multiple footprints facing different directions, the floor lay undisturbed.

Ruth crouched at the open trapdoor and shouted down, "Are you sure you don't need us down there?"

"We're fine," Zoe told her, raking at a spiderweb she had walked into. She shivered involuntarily.

Like the officers before them, Willa and Zoe played their flashlight beams around the cellar. It was one room, one large room, lined with shelves and knickknacks, and all of it draped in sheets like furniture in a boarded-up house. But here, the sheets were made of dust and cobwebs.

"Isn't there any kind of light down here? Did all those school kids have to carry their own flashlights?" Zoe called out.

"You know," Ardell mused, "we used to have a camping lantern down there. One of those two-mantle ones. Look on the table in front of you. The fuel's probably all evaporated by now, though."

Ardell sat on the floor above the cellar, her feet resting down a couple of steps. She sidled over to make room for Ruth beside her. The faces of browsing customers stared curiously over their shoulders before passing on.

"I've got it," Zoe declared, lifting the lantern by its gritty handle. "How about some matches?"

"They should be there. Don't forget to pump up the pressure in that lantern first, before you light it." To Ruth, Ardell added, "Those matches are probably mildewed, you know."

The lantern was bright enough that it hurt to look at it. It threw the shadows into retreat and cast a white light that made the dusty cavern feel like an operating room.

"What are you looking for?" Willa asked.

"I don't know." Calling up to Ardell, Zoe inquired, "How many people do you think passed through here?"

"Slaves on the run? Oh, we really don't know. The stories say probably forty or more. Never more than two or three at any one time."

"Where would they go if someone opened that trapdoor? Wasn't there always supposed to be another way out, like in mole holes?"

Ruth said, "Another way out? You're under the ground down there, Zoe. Where would there be another way out? There was a glass case up here. It was such a heavy piece of furniture that no one thought it was movable. Camouflage was the idea, not another doorway."

Beside Zoe, Willa muttered, "Um-hmm." And raised her voice to ask, "And whatever happened to that magical glass case, Ruth?"

"As a matter of fact, I think Franklin carted it on up that mountain so's he could display his carving in his living room. He thought he was some authentic woodsman. But no one could ever tell what his carvings were."

Ardell added, "It was a good thing modern art came around when it did. Then he could say it was an abstract rendition." The sisters laughed.

Zoe blew the dust off some children's books and delved into a box of old tin toys. "You could have some valuable stuff down here. For a collector, I mean."

"I reckon we do. It'll all get sorted out in time, I imagine," Ruth said. "Say, do you see any Christmas decorations down there? We used to have a wonderful big wreath that we put up every year, and it occurs to me that I haven't seen it in quite some time."

"We'll check," Willa said, with some doubt coloring her voice. She sneezed as she lifted a small box to inspect the larger one beneath it.

Zoe was tapping the walls at periodic intervals, but nothing sounded hollow. Mostly she was doing a good job of scraping her knuckles. "This room is big," she said doubtfully, looking around, "but it's not big enough to go all the way under the entire store above. I never heard of a foundation like that."

"What was that, Zoe?" Ruth called down. "Did you find the wreath?"

"Not yet. I was saying that the room down here doesn't seem as large as what's over it. How could a building larger than the foundation—"

"Oh, that's where you're wrong," Ardell interrupted. "When this place was first built, it was erected over a stream. The front part of the store was really a porch on stilts. People would water their horses down below, turn them loose to graze in the meadow, and then climb outside steps in order to enter the main building. Maybe ten or fifteen years after the building was put up, that outside part was enclosed, and the Ordinary was enlarged. The land was filled in down below when the stream was diverted for farmland. So what's now the front of the Ordinary wasn't a part of the original building at all. We have drawings somewhere of what it used to look like. Well, photocopies of drawings. Someone found them in a book and sent them to us. When people chide us for changing the structure and building the lunch counter, we tell them we weren't the first to fiddle with the place."

"What ever happened to those drawings?" Ruth asked. "We were going to frame them and hang them, weren't we? You didn't go and lose them, did you?"

"I'm telling you," Willa said, although there was no triumph in her voice, "it was all a bunch of hooey. For something that existed mainly in the imagination, it's stuck around a long time, kind of like those stories of snakes lying in wait inside the arms of winter coats in the department stores."

"It sounds as if you want it to be real." Zoe said as she tapped again at the wall.

"The Underground Railroad? I do. And I want Santa Claus to be real, too. It ain't gonna happen, though, babe."

Zoe was behind the stairs when a particular tap sounded different to her ears. "Listen to this."

She knocked for Willa's benefit. Both of them cocked their heads, listening intently. Willa tapped at the wall where she stood and then shook her head. "Sounds the same to me."

"I'm not so sure."

"Besides, look at the location in terms of where the store's standing. That wall is under the store. According to the stories, the way out would be an underground pathway to an outbuilding, like a barn or a springhouse. Or even to the outside. If you go out there, you end up back under the Ordinary. What good would that have done anyone?"

No dust had been disturbed on the floor. There were neither mouse droppings nor tracks. Cobwebs with old corpses hanging in them were the only sign of life. Zoe sighed and turned around.

Beneath the stairs was a large, round bundle wrapped in dusty plastic. "I might have your wreath here, Ruth."

"Well, hand it on up. You wouldn't happen to see some lights to go with it, would you?"

"Could be. Let's take care of the wreath first." Zoe headed back for the stairs, and as she lifted the heavy wreath toward the opening in the floor above, a foreign hand reached between the sisters.

Sam Bennett grinned shyly. "Let me take that," he offered as he easily hauled up the wreath.

"Say," he said diffidently, "do you think I could have a look down there?" He laid the wreath on the floor.

"Sam!" Wyatt called from somewhere near the door. "We've got to get back to work."

"In a minute," Sam said over his shoulder. To Ardell and

Ruth he explained, "I was one of those kids who had a tour down there, back when. Could I go down again?"

Ardell gestured with her hand as she made room for a third body on the old stairs.

Clattering down the wooden steps, Sam stopped at the bottom for a quick look around.

"Pretty impressive, huh?" Willa asked with more than a touch of irony, raising her eyebrows. "Is it everything you remembered?"

At first, Sam said nothing. Then he took a deep breath. "You could keep a dog kenneled down here," he said, nodding to himself.

"But why would you want to?" Willa asked.

Embarrassed, Sam reddened. "Just a thought. It seems to be how I evaluate every place I see, I guess. If it's watertight, not too stuffy or windy, if there's room for a dog to turn around, stand up, lie down . . . Those are the things I notice about a place."

"Sounds like how you're going to get to be with that trapped cat," Willa said, elbowing Zoe.

"Do you remember what you learned down here?" Zoe asked Sam.

He shrugged. "Not really."

Zoe turned to the women at the top of the stairs and asked, "What kinds of stories did you tell those kids who came on field trips from school?"

Ruth and Ardell looked at each other. It was Ardell who explained, "Sometimes we dressed in costumes and pretended it was the 1840s, back before the Civil War. Then we'd tell the children how dangerous it was to smuggle slaves out of the South. Virginia was a border state then, remember, and West Virginia hadn't seceded yet. Slaves would make their way to the North, stopping at sites like this along the way. Once here, they'd get food and water and clothing, if there was any, and be helped on their way when the road was clear."

Willa snorted. "I wish. I wish it had been so easy."

"Easy?" Ruth squared her shoulders. "Easy? Why, there was nothing easy about it. It meant slipping away from the only place you'd known, striking out for a place you'd only heard of, a place that could be days or months away, for all you knew. It meant escaping from the people who'd been recruited to catch you, people who did that for a living! And it meant looking over your shoulder the entire time, not knowing, even when you reached the free states, just when or if the hand of a slave catcher might come down on you. And if you made it to Canada, it meant starting from nothing, all on your own. There was nothing easy about it!"

On the other side of the stairs, Willa lifted up a dusty box of colored lights. She sneezed. "Whoever hid down here, I hope they didn't have asthma!"

Zoe waited until Willa and Sam were up the stairs before she extinguished the lantern, retrieved both flashlights, and followed. She looked at the heavy trapdoor as the sisters lowered it into place, and it rested level with the floor. A wide brass ring, which fit into a carved hollow in the door, served as its handle. Once it was laid flat, a braided rug was flung into place over top. And it was as if the room beneath did not exist at all.

It was one of those mornings that presage winter, crisp and bright and cold. The mist on the windshield would soon be frost, given the passage of a few more days and the loss of a few more degrees. Overnight, leaves had blown from trees, plucked by gigantic handfuls, and scattered. They snapped satisfyingly underfoot.

As she squeegeed off the car windows, Zoe listened to the river, its chatter from far down the mountain like a familiar song. In a peaceful mood, she drove toward Sinksville. Talking aloud in the Chevy, she reviewed what she had learned from Ethan.

As she had surmised, there was no telling how long Susan Rourke had been missing. The last sighting of her had been three days before the estimated time of Patrick Rourke's death. One of the mechanics at DeSoto's garage had checked Susan's radiator when she bought gas. After that, as far as the police knew, Susan had disappeared. But no one could pinpoint when. The gas tank in the van had been almost full.

There had been no fingerprints on Patrick Rourke's shotgun. It had been wiped clean.

Ethan had brought Zoe the promised copy of the list of the contents of Patrick Rourke's truck, the cab of which had also been wiped clean of prints. She had left the inventory on her desk but remembered most of it: torn and multiply-folded highway maps, Styrofoam cups, fast-food wrappers, extra fuses, a flashlight with no batteries, a crowbar under the seat. The list also included a locked toolbox in the bed of the truck and twenty-six loose shotgun shells. The only unusual item she spotted was a convenience store plastic travel mug with a few swallows of moonshine left in it. No bottle or jug had been found at his home, in his work locker, or in his truck.

Zoe followed Laurel's directions up the narrow back road to the small parking area she had visited only two days earlier with the search party. She pulled in next to the Saturn.

The wind hit her in the face as she found the path that led up to the house. It was a force that took no pause for breath, seeming neither to diminish nor gust in its strength. It found the seams in her jacket and pushed its way inside.

She raised her face to the sun and marched up the narrow path, grinning at the wind's strength, while leaves swooped around her like countless sparrows on speed.

Even searching for Laurel Taylor's house, she almost walked right past it. The dwelling was set back from the path, nestled in a drop so sharp that she looked down on most of the shake roof. A weathered wooden tower rose among tall, misshapen firs that masked its windows and camouflaged a small balcony. The natural siding blended chameleonlike into the mountainside far behind it. For a moment, Zoe simply stood and marveled. Like an optical illusion, the house seemed to disappear, and then she could pick it out again.

She could not see an entrance from her vantage, but she followed a narrower trail that ran alongside the house. She rapped on the wide beamed door.

"Laurel?"

The loud, discordant slam of what sounded like a sledge-hammer falling on piano keys made her hesitate, back up a step. A few moments later the door was flung open so hard it hit the inside wall. There was little light inside, and it was hard to distinguish shadow from substance. For an instant, Zoe felt an inexplicable tingle of terror cross her spine, and without conscious thought, her feet poised to take flight.

Then the moment passed, and rationality reasserted itself. Zoe's eyes made out the shape of a head over a plaid flannel shirt worn, as the day before, loosely over jeans. Work boots poked out from under ragged hems.

Laurel Taylor took a step nearer the light and sniffled deeply. Her gray eyes were tinged with red, her round face blotchy with recently shed tears. Again, she held her head tilted slightly so that her hair fell forward and shielded her face from view.

"I forgot you were coming," she said, sniffling again and raising her head slightly so that her bruised eyes surveyed Zoe without inviting sympathy.

"Would you rather I came back some other time?"

The hair covered Laurel's face as she shook her head. "No. You came all this way. You might as well come on in."

As Zoe entered the narrow room, she heard a door slam. Laurel pressed her lips together. "Men! Why do women have anything to do with them?"

Zoe had no ready answer for that one, assuming the question to be rhetorical.

"Well, we might as well talk out back," Laurel offered lamely. "I hope you don't mind the wind."

"Nope. As a matter of fact, I love it." The force of it would soon try to make her eat her words, but Zoe was not about to take back what she had said.

Laurel led her through the old house and out to the back deck, which was as wide and open as the house was narrow and cramped. It spanned the width of the house and stretched out into the air over the mountain like an eagle spreading its wings. Wide wooden planks ended in midair, with nothing but gold, flame, and green both far beneath and rolling away over distant hills, until the trees receded into indistinguishable background.

A sudden sensation of vertigo hit Zoe, and she took a step back.

"It affects lots of people that way at first," Laurel observed. "But the dizziness goes away after a while. You never do get your breath back, though. You like it? On clear days, you can almost see Maryland to the north. And Virginia's right over there."

"It's magnificent!" Zoe exclaimed, although the adjective hardly seemed to do justice to the panorama that challenged the eyes and filled the heart.

To the right, a crude roof and a latticework lean-to had been added against the outer wall of the house. Inside the structure sat an upright piano, presumably the one Zoe had heard when she knocked.

Seeing where Zoe's eye fell, Laurel said, "I can wheel it out into the sunshine when I feel like it. Sometimes I hold concerts for the bears. I take it into the house in the winter, though. Otherwise, it would really warp. I don't think the sun and rain do it too much good as it is."

Zoe walked toward the piano only because it seemed safer than walking back toward the edge of the deck. Laurel followed, and from the corner of her eye, Zoe saw Laurel's hand go to her mouth.

At the same instant, Zoe spotted a pregnancy test kit on the top of the piano. Just above the keys lay the tester, clearly showing a negative result.

Seeking to preserve the other woman's privacy, she made an abrupt turn and took a couple of bravado steps toward the edge of the deck. "Did you build this yourself?"

"Pretty much. We used to have a small porch back here, but it was kind of sliding down the mountain. I needed something sturdier. And I wanted something bigger."

"It must have been a lot of work, required a lot of support from below." Zoe said it admiringly, but she could see from Laurel's reaction that the other woman figured she was being challenged.

Laurel turned sullen and dipped her head again. "I read up on it. Even watched some tapes from the library over in Russell Creek."

"I've done that, too. Borrowed tapes, I mean. There was a lot about old houses I never knew before I bought mine. Heck, there's still a lot I don't know. But building this is some accomplishment! It's beautiful!"

Laurel nodded, relenting a bit. She gestured toward the picnic table tucked at the rear of the deck, sheltered against the house. "Why don't you sit down? I'll go get us something warm to drink."

But instead of sitting at the indicated bench, Zoe followed Laurel as she left the deck. Leaning against the kitchen doorway, Zoe watched while Laurel moved self-consciously to the sink, where she took two mugs from the dish drainer. "Hot chocolate okay? I could make instant coffee, if you want."

"No, hot chocolate's fine."

A quick smile flitted across Laurel's face, turning her eyes to liquid mercury and softening her features. "Dorsey says it's cocoa. I say cocoa is what you add to sugar and milk to make it into . . ."

Suddenly stricken, she turned from Zoe, and her voice faded away. She ran water into a kettle. Zoe studied Laurel's stiff back. She had revealed something she wasn't supposed to.

It was not hard for Zoe to assume that Dorsey was the one who had something to do with the flat tire the day before and the pregnancy test today. She did not yet see what any of that had to do with Susan Rourke's disappearance or Patrick Rourke's murder, if anything.

But Zoe wanted to know why Laurel was protecting Dorsey's anonymity so fiercely.

She glanced toward the rest of the house. "Ardell Lamb and Ruth Cook say your grandfather was something of a character around here. They said he hauled some big glass case up here. Could I have a look at it?"

Zoe saw the quick flutter of a smile cross Laurel's features as the terror of mentioning Dorsey's name slipped away. "Grandpap Franklin. And his daddy Franklin, too. Both of them are like legends in these hills. Great-Grandpap Franklin, he staked claim to just about all of them. And what he couldn't claim, he bought."

She took two packets of hot chocolate mix and emptied them into the mugs. Then she brushed past Zoe, exiting the kitchen through a narrow doorway Zoe had not noticed.

Laurel looked over her shoulder at Zoe. "This is what we used to call the parlor. Before the tower got built, this is where Grandpap Franklin kept all his treasures. Mostly things he scrounged from around the hills. Did you happen to see those animals carved from coal at the Ordinary? Well, my Grandpap's daddy, he carved the first ones. Then Grandpap did it. The ones they sell now, they're made by machine, and not in West Virginia either."

She led the way to a corner of the room. The air was chilly and smelled of wool and dampness. "The dogs like to sleep in here," she said. "They're off running now, with—They're off running now."

She lifted her face. "Up this ladder is the tower. Grandpap Franklin built it so's he could spy on people before they got here. Way back when, the only way in was across the mountains on foot from Sinksville. And the most likely people to be coming were revenuers."

She sank down on an afghan-covered sofa and grinned in remembrance. "Grandpap used to tell us stories about back then. They always ended with the revenuers hightailing it back to Sinksville!"

Her smile turned sad. "Grandpap used to tell me, 'don't you and your sister go selling my land now.' He said that was what made him rich.

"And we haven't sold it, either. Not one little bit of it. Not even the mineral rights. It's probably the only spot in West Virginia you can say that about. Trouble is, I'm rich in land, but I can't get my hands on any money."

"You own all the land between here and Sinksville?" Zoe perched on the edge of the sofa.

"Yeah. And quite a bit in Sinksville, too. Well, Susan and I do together. We talk about selling it sometimes, but then we think about Grandpap Franklin, and we kind of back off. Aunt Ruth and Aunt Ardell run the Ordinary, but you know, it's always belonged to my family. There are a few other properties in Sinksville, too. And there's a dry cleaner's about ten miles from here. I don't know how we got that one, unless Grandpap took it in payment for moonshine.

"I don't know how I got started on all this. . ."

"The glass case."

"Oh, yeah. Sometimes, it seems like I don't talk to anyone for so long, I just run on and on. I know, you're thinking about him, but he's really not such great company lately. Or maybe it's me." She sighed.

"Well, come on up the ladder. The case is up there."

She hauled herself off the sofa, and Zoe followed. They climbed up rungs discolored by the oils of countless palms going hand-over-hand along their widths. An open square cut in the ceiling eventually revealed a room literally among the trees. Tall firs shaded the windows. The walls had been whitewashed, and a faded map showing Sinksville, mountains, streams, and this house, as well as several trails, was drawn directly on the wall between two windows that looked out toward Sinksville, hidden behind the intervening geography. Two huge pillows, warped by bodies and settled filling, were tossed into one corner. Beneath a window that looked down on the path Zoe had come up stood the glass case.

The case was made mostly of wood. The top and the side facing the room were unbroken sheets of glass, perhaps four feet long. Inside the case were several unidentifiable shapes carved from coal, as well as some arrowheads, marine fossils, eagle feathers, and animal canines that looked as if someone had attempted scrimshaw upon them.

Laurel hid her face behind her hair as she explained, "My brother Tuck and Susan and I helped Grandpap dig up those fossils. They're mostly shells, but there are a couple of plants, too. He said they were treasures enough to go in the case, and they've been there ever since."

"How did he ever manage to carry this thing up here?"

Laurel shrugged. "By mule or donkey, I guess. Piece by piece. And then he had to bring it up through the hole in the floor or in through the windows. He did a little of both, from what I heard. He'd been sitting up in this room, watching for revenuers, and he decided he needed something to look at besides the view. There's a big slide over on Rainy Mountain across the way, and people would have to go over that to get here, so Grandpap didn't have to keep a real close watch. He said he was sampling his brew up here one day, and it just occurred to him that he needed that case from the Ordinary."

Zoe bent closer to the case. "Is this maple?"

"Yeah, I think so."

Zoe's attention was drawn downward. The case rested on four squat legs, carved into what Zoe imagined were supposed to signify lions' feet. She turned to Laurel to marvel, and then turned back to the case. "I thought it would be on casters!"

"Not that I've ever known."

"But I thought Ardell and Ruth said it covered the trapdoor to the basement. Maybe I was assuming that it would have to have wheels if they were sliding it back and forth over that door."

"The Underground Railroad," Laurel nodded. "I've heard that story so often, I get confused about when the Civil War was. I always picture Aunt Ardell and Aunt Ruth involved right in the middle of the smuggling."

"They did say they used to wear costumes from those days."

Laurel nodded again. "They get all het up about it, even now. That little room is their pride and joy. They used to show it off to anyone they could talk into going down! It was fixed up so nice, with a table and chairs and cots. There was even plastic food set out, as if some runaway slaves had just left. I used to love playing down there! Lately, I haven't even thought about it.

"We'd better head back down to the kitchen or that water will all boil away, and I won't even be able to blame him for it!" She shot Zoe a grin and disappeared, like the White Rabbit, down the hole.

Somewhat more slowly, Zoe followed. Her mind was busy chewing over the importance of the land. With Patrick Rourke dead, Susan and Laurel would have sole control of it again. But if Susan lay dead somewhere, then there was a good likelihood that everything belonged to Laurel. What dreams did she harbor for all the acres that folded around the house like rumpled blankets? Or was Dorsey the one with the dreams?

While drinking the hot chocolate, Zoe asked, "Do you have any idea where Patrick's traps are?"

She did not confide it to Laurel, but she wanted to make sure that Susan was not lying out of hearing distance somewhere, her ankle pulverized in a trap, her eyes slowly losing the gleam inside as her life slipped away, the near fate of the orange tabby.

"I'm pretty sure. Well, not sure exactly, but I know he always kept a map of where he put his traps because he kept moving the things. The question is, where did he keep that map? My guess would be that it's in the shed down by the parking area. He used to keep some stuff in there, and if he's trapping that close to the house . . . I'm lucky it wasn't one of the dogs in that trap. They go ranging all over these hills, and Patrick knew it! But he had to keep trapping, wouldn't listen when people tried to talk him out of it. Even Patrick thought it was cruel, but he didn't want to hear any of it. You hate to say it about another person, especially someone dead, but I think the pain of others made him feel real good."

She frowned and clamped her lips together.

"Did the police ask you about his traps?"

Laurel's eyes shifted to the left for a couple of seconds. "Not that I can recall. Not important, I guess. They did take tire tracks from down there at the shed. Well, imprints, you know? And I guess they went through the shed, too, now that I think about it. They asked me if he stored stuff around here. So, on second thought, we might not find that map."

They decided to look anyway. It was a starting place.

The wind at their backs hurried them along as effectively as an open palm above the waist. The sky remained the cloudless blue of a kindergarten finger painting, with the sun a brilliant circle in the corner.

The trail was several inches below the surrounding ground, a testament to its use over the years. It was rocky and uneven, though, and even a glimpse at the expanse of the sky or the mountains risked a stubbed toe at best or a good chance for a steep dive. Zoe forced herself to keep her attention mostly on her feet.

It seemed a much shorter distance down than it had been going up. Laurel led the way to the shed and placed her hands on her hips, surveying it from the outside.

It looked much the same as it had two days before, with bales of straw opened and slowly decaying on the dirt, a small cache of road salt, the rusting snowplow.

"Where would he keep a map in here?"

Laurel breathed heavily. "Let me think a moment." The wind lifted her wool shirt jacket, which she wore unbuttoned, and she raised her head to the sun.

A moment later the answer came to her, and she smiled at Zoe. "Not in this place, I think. I think he used our playhouse!"

"Playhouse?"

"Yeah. It's just over the hill. My mama built it for Susan and Tuck and me. She told us it was like a springhouse."

"A springhouse?" Zoe repeated. Her Gran, whose cabin had no electricity, kept a springhouse.

Laurel misread Zoe's expression as incomprehension. "Yeah! A springhouse. That's where people used to store their milk and butter and stuff before there was refrigeration. There must have been one over at your place if it's a hundred years old! There would be a spring running through it, and it would stay cool even in hot weather. Anyway, Mama built this one for us on a creek that was already dry. But she built it low over the creek bed, just like a real springhouse, except with a real floor. She told us it was for play, but it was where she sent us when—"

Her lips clamped together again, and she blinked back tears as she turned away from Zoe. Pointing with her chin, she continued, "It's just over the hill." And started off.

Zoe hurried to catch up. "Did you hide out there from your father?"

Laurel's eyes were watery and wide when she stole a look at her companion. Her shoulders had hunched, and her hands were balled into fists.

As casually as Zoe could, with her breath coming faster as Laurel put on more and more speed, she added, "I've seen some of the things people can do to each other, especially when there's alcohol involved." She tried to say it in her dispassionate, professional voice, the one that heard nothing too far from the norm.

Laurel's mouth twisted before she nodded. "Your dad that way, too?"

For a brief instant, knowing it would make her trust Zoe more, perhaps be more open, Zoe contemplated lying to her. But she could not, would not. She figured Laurel must have been lied to enough in her lifetime already. "No, he wasn't. But I've met a few like that over the years."

Laurel sighed and nodded. "I always tried to make him happy. But I never could. Especially after Tucker drowned." Tears began tracking down her cheeks, and her nose grew red and runny. She sniffled.

"I know it was 'cause he blamed himself. Same as I blame myself for not being there to help. Same as I blame myself for not being better to make it easier on him. I tell myself it's not my fault. But that doesn't stop the feelings. They don't go away."

Zoe slipped an arm around Laurel's shoulders. "I'll bet Patrick was like your dad when he drank, wasn't he?"

She nodded and wiped her nose with her fist. Zoe did not have anything better to offer her.

Laurel said, "Except Patrick was mostly like that all the time. Susan says he isn't, but that's how he's always seemed to me. On edge, like, you know? He could smile and make all nice to people when he wanted to, but his real face, the one he showed when he wasn't thinking about it, it was mean. My daddy wasn't like that. He really wasn't. He was always sorry afterward. And he could be so nice sometimes. Patrick, he was never sorry. He'd say he was, but you never believed him." She stepped away from Zoe's arm and began walking again.

Zoe hung back, internally arguing with herself. Eventually, Laurel noticed, and after slowing, turned back. Zoe knew it was none of her business, but Laurel seemed vulnerable, like Susan. She was physically more solid, but Zoe did not see it reflected in the strength of her self-confidence. The former Justice Department investigator had minded her own business where Laurel's sister had been concerned, and now she pushed herself to ask, "Does *he* treat you that way?" She had unconsciously fallen into Laurel's speech quirk. "Dorsey?"

Her face paled. "He'd never!" Laurel declared in a shocked tone.

"I'd help you if he did. Any way I could."

This time Laurel laughed. "You think I'd let him into my house if he did? You think I'd let my dogs go out with him? I've seen him catch a fly with his bare hands and take it outside so he could let it go rather than swat it. I told him a long time ago, if he takes a swipe at me, it's the last one he's taking. And he agreed with me!" She shook her head and repeated, "He'd never!"

She continued shaking her head, and her eyes turned hard at the same time her voice grew low and clipped. "I'm not my sister, Zoe. I love her very much, but I'm not her."

Zoe nodded soberly. "I didn't mean to offend."

Laurel tossed her head and then immediately tucked it between her breasts. The wall of hair fell into place. "You didn't exactly say anything to offend me. I shouldn't have jumped on you like that."

"You hardly jumped at all."

Laurel raised her chin and smiled, her gait lengthening to a stride. "I'd forgotten all about the springhouse. Isn't it a wonder how things can slip your mind and then you suddenly stumble on them again?"

"So the police didn't ask you about the springhouse?"

"How could they? I didn't remember it myself. And I doubt if anyone else told them about it. Who else would know but us?"

"But Patrick knew about it."

"Because Susan told him. They used to meet there, I think. Way back. No one liked Patrick much. Ruth and Ardell wouldn't let him come calling at the Ordinary, so Susan had to meet him wherever she could."

Technically, Zoe knew, the police should be told about the springhouse. It should have been searched already, and if the two women found anything in there pertaining to Patrick Rourke's murder, they could be obstructing the official investigation, tampering with evidence. None of it would reflect nicely on Zoe, the one who knew better.

But she said nothing because Zoe had a sudden feeling that they would find Susan hiding in that springhouse. The more

Laurel described it, the more Zoe saw it as a safe, secure refuge, where a scared and maybe hurt fugitive could gather her wits and rest. Zoe did not want the police to discover Susan first. And she had no desire to turn Susan in. She only wanted to find her alive. Her imagination took her no further than that.

The roof of the springhouse was already camouflaged in fallen leaves, and Zoe and Laurel crunched loudly through the dry streambed. Even someone wearing earplugs surely would have been alerted to their coming.

Laurel reached up to the plank door and then hesitated before turning to Zoe. "I haven't been here for a while. Would you mind going first?"

Her hand dropped away, and Zoe's replaced it on the latch. The older woman waited a moment until Laurel slipped behind her so the door would not open in her face. The warped planks swung open on new leather hinges and revealed a musty, dark cave.

Laurel stood on tiptoe to peer over Zoe's shoulder. "What's in there?"

"I can't tell. Do you know if there's a match anywhere in there?"

"Just to the right of the door, where you'd expect to find a light switch? There should be a little basket nailed to the wall. It's got matches and candles. Or it used to. Did you just feel something cold go by?"

Zoe turned from the darkness. "What do you mean, something cold?"

Laurel's face had gone pale. "Nothing, I guess. Just my imagination."

"Do you mean a ghost?" Hadn't Ruth said she'd seen Tuck Taylor's ghost in these hills?

"Couldn't be, huh?"

"I've never seen one or felt one, Laurel." Zoe was a skeptic of the first degree. "Have you?" She kept her tone conversational, not wanting to imply that her mind was closed to the possibility.

Laurel set her lips in a thin line and nodded. "He used to come banging on the windows, but I wouldn't let him in. The dogs would be howling, with the hair on their backs standing up, and I wouldn't let him in."

"Who? Patrick?"

"No, Tuck. My brother who drowned. They never found his body, and he was never laid to rest. I know I shouldn't be afraid of him. He's just a spirit. Besides, I never did him any harm. But he's walking these woods. And all I know is he scares me. I thought maybe he'd be living in here, since I didn't let him into the house."

Zoe took a deep breath, reached with her right hand into the black pit of the little wood hut, and closed her fingers around a candle stub and a limp box of matches.

Luckily, the matches were wooden, and dry, and the first one she flicked against the door flared up. With a suddenly jittery hand, she lit the candle and held it before her as she stepped up and into the springhouse.

Laurel grasped hold of the back of Zoe's jacket and followed her inside. Spiderwebs threw writhing shadows on the walls and across the broad shelves. A big-eared mouse stared from a corner before darting into a hole. Acorns and leaves lay scattered across the wood like rice after a wedding. The place was damp and very cold.

The raised candle revealed oiled traps gleaming softly on the top shelves on each side of the little house. A couple of old rags were heaped at one end of the right-hand shelf, and a tackle box fastened with cobwebs sat against the wall of the left-hand bench. There was no trace of Susan, no sign that she had ever been to the place at all. Zoe searched the small space again, not wanting to believe her eyes, certain that she must have overlooked the woman, disappointed that her hunch had failed to pay out.

Laurel pointed to the tackle box. "That was my shelf. We'd lie in here and tell stories to each other. I liked it here because I got to be with Tuck and Susan. They didn't always have time for me otherwise. When it got real bad, Mama came, too."

Zoe handed her the candle and went to work on the tackle box. It opened easily enough. Inside were tools, pieces of hardware, nuts, bolts, and assorted brackets and doodads she could not identify. On the bottom of the box was a small, damp tablet and a pencil stub. The top sheet of the tablet showed a crude map with a number of Xs marked, mostly along the dry creek bed that held the springhouse.

"Pay dirt," she said, just as a soft rush of air snuffed out the candle flame.

The rest of the traps were empty. It took some time and some luck, but Laurel and Zoe found every one of the traps indicated on the map—except for the one Zoe had recovered, complete with cat, days earlier. As they discovered each empty one, they tripped it with downed tree limbs or whatever was handy, and left it in place.

As they trudged contentedly back up the hillside toward the parking area, a sense of a day's work well done shared between them, two big dogs bounded over the ridge. Shepherd mixes, with dark brown saddles over short, tan fur, they also sported tails and legs cast from extra-large molds.

Laurel crouched down to welcome them both, letting them lick her face until there was no doubt in Zoe's mind that she would be permanently chapped. Done with their greeting, they panted while they eyed Zoe, tongues hanging out, sides heaving.

"These are my boys," Laurel announced proudly. "This one's Goodness and that's Mercy. I call them that because they follow me all the days of my life. If I had a third one, I'd call him Shirley.

You know, Shirley, Goodness, and Mercy . . ." She smiled slightly, waiting to see if Zoe got the joke.

Obligingly, Zoe groaned, then asked, "Laurel, do you have any idea how often Patrick would check his traps?"

She shrugged, resting a hand on the back of each dog. "I have no idea. Is it important? I mean, he could hardly check them after he was dead, could he?"

"My little cat was in that trap for about three or four days, my vet thinks. It could have been longer. I found him soon after Patrick must have died. Let's say it was twelve hours later at the outside. If Patrick hadn't checked his traps the day before he died, why hadn't he?"

"Because he was busy kidnapping my sister?"

"Then why set the traps at all if he knew he was going to be driving to Beverage to kidnap your sister?"

"Because he was a stinking drunk is why! You keep talking like you expect him to make sense, but when he drank—" She shrugged. "It's simple! He got drunk, and he decided to go after Susan. He wasn't thinking about his traps at all!"

The dogs gave short, gruff barks and studied Laurel's face for a clue as to what was upsetting their leader. Goodness growled low in his throat, his eyes moving to Zoe.

"Maybe. Maybe." She felt her insides knot up, and she studied the sky, not sure she should be thinking out loud in front of Laurel. Nonetheless, she decided to ask, "How did he know she was in Beverage, Laurel? How many people knew where she was? How did he know where to find her?"

Laurel's eyes grew wide and defiant. "He didn't follow me, if that's what you're still thinking! And I sure as heck didn't tell him!"

"I know." They had reached the far end of the parking area, and Zoe leaned casually against the dented fender of her car. "But who else knew, Laurel? How else did he manage to find her?"

"I don't know who else she might have called!"

"Who told you? Did she call you?"

Laurel scuffed her shoe in the gravel and dirt. "Susan called me at the Ordinary. She knows I do my shopping there at a set time every week. We used to meet there sometimes. She was afraid to call me at home, afraid Patrick might somehow tap into the line to the house, it being so isolated and all. He wasn't at the Ordinary! He didn't overhear!"

"Did you tell Ruth and Ardell where she was?"

"Susan had already talked to them. They helped to raise us! There's no way they'd tell anyone where Susan was! Especially Patrick! They never did like him. No, no way!"

"Well, then, who else knew? Did you tell Dorsey?"

The dogs' ears pricked up at the mention of a name they knew.

Laurel raised her head, shocked. "He'd never!"

"I'd like to talk to him. Do you think he's up at the house?"

"I don't know! I'm not his keeper!" She shouted belligerently, and the dogs danced and shuffled at her feet, crowding close to her and moving away, licking their lips in anxiety. In a lower tone, Laurel said, "He didn't tell Patrick a thing."

"How do you think Patrick found her?"

Laurel's chin raised. "Maybe she called him. Have you thought of that? She was all the time going back to him. He'd cry, and she'd believe him, and then it would start all over again. She told me she was going to be strong this time, but she wasn't! I try not to blame her. I really do! But why'd she have to be so stupid?"

Of course, it was possible, Zoe knew, but if that were the case, then why hadn't she simply returned to him, the way she apparently had before?

"Laurel, as far as you know, did your sister have a special friend? A man friend? A protector, perhaps, someone willing to kill to make sure Patrick never hurt Susan again?" But, Zoe knew even as she asked the lame question, if that were the case, where was he? The man should be stepping forward claiming self-defense, and Susan should be with him, backing him up. She would not have disappeared.

Laurel snorted. "You mean some lover? The cops asked me that, too. No way. After a man treats you so bad, are you going to go out and find another one? No, not even Susan. There was a guy at the mall over in Russell Creek who tried to hit on her once when we went to the movies, and she was so terrified that Patrick might find out, we left without even seeing the movie."

"Well, when you talked to your sister, or when you saw her in Beverage, did she ever mention that there was someone new in her life?"

Laurel smiled ironically. "Yeah, now that you mention it. She did say she'd met somebody she liked."

"Who?"

"You."

Zoe didn't know what it was she wasn't supposed to learn about Dorsey, but without saying a thing, without asking or being invited, she accompanied Laurel and the dogs back to her house, determined to find out.

In her mind she pictured a six-foot-tall mountain man, broad shouldered and bearded, with more muscle than mind. He probably spoke in grunts slightly more articulate than Sylvester Stallone, chewed tobacco, and carried a shotgun in one hand and a liquor jug in the other. Even as she resented the hillbilly stereotype, her mind presented it to her.

Not able to tell Zoe she was no longer welcome, Laurel reluctantly opened the door to the house. She did not call out a warning or a greeting. The dogs muscled past them, scrabbled through the kitchen, and Zoe imagined, plopped onto the sofa in the room where they slept.

"Hey, babe."

Zoe turned in the direction of the voice to see sun streaming in behind the shadowed outline of a man. If this was the infamous Dorsey, he met none of her stereotypical expectations. He was slight, about as tall as Laurel, and his hair, with a few wavy detours, fell in a cascade to his shoulders. A heavy moustache blurred the outline of his upper lip.

He held a can of beer or cola in his hand. Given the quality of the light, Zoe could not tell which it was. He took a swig and punched the can toward her. "This your detective?"

"Not mine," Laurel said sullenly.

Zoe extended her hand. "Zoe Kergulin."

He didn't shake it. Instead he gripped the can with both hands and toyed with the metal tab on top. "Dorsey."

"Laurel said you were out with the dogs." She let her arm fall to her side.

He nodded slowly. "I like to take 'em out for a little exercise now and then. I love to see them running full out."

"Are you from around here?"

"What's with all the questions?" Laurel asked in tones more desperate than the situation warranted.

"It's okay, babe," Dorsey soothed, in a voice that also dismissed. "My family has a place not far from here. We moved away a long time ago, when my parents split up. And now I'm back." Zoe saw a flicker of teeth. "How's that?"

"Frankly," she said, "it could use some embellishment."

"Yeah? I'll have to work on it. You want to come sit down, or are we all going to just stand here?"

They trooped out to the deck. It was in shade and very cold. Dorsey had a fire going in a barrel, and they pulled plastic chairs close to it.

As Zoe's toes thawed, she wriggled them. All the while, her eyes carefully moved across the landscape and back, surveying Dorsey and Laurel.

Laurel glanced up briefly. "Dorsey, Zoe and I found a place that I used to play in when I was a kid. Patrick kept his traps and stuff in there. And we found a map so we knew where each one of his traps was set."

"Hand it over, and I'll go take care of 'em." He smiled wickedly. "Patrick used to keep his traps in that shed down by the parking lot. But I kind of monkey wrenched 'em. I had no idea they were still around."

"We already took care of them." Laurel smiled a bit and kept her chin up this time. "Remember I told you that when I met Zoe, she told me about rescuing a cat in one of Patrick's traps?"

"Yeah. It's a good thing you found it before the dogs did. That cat going to be all right?"

Zoe nodded. "He may lose a leg. But he's at the vet's now, and he's getting good care."

"We could take him, I guess," Dorsey said, scratching at his nose with the tab of the can. "But I'd worry about the dogs getting him. I'm not sure how they'd do with a cat, especially one who might not be so good jumping away from them. Maybe we could keep him down in the bedroom, though, huh, babe?"

"That's okay," Zoe interposed quickly. "He'll be coming home with me as soon as he's well enough. Laurel, it's probably best that we turn that map over to the police. They may have no use for it, but I think they're the ones who should have it."

She shrugged noncommittally. "I have a meeting with a detective sometime tomorrow. I could give it to her then."

"Great."

Dorsey tilted his head. "Say, aren't you the one having that thing with the sheriff? Didn't he leave his wife because of you?"

Laurel gave him a quick, harmless kick in the shin, a warning.

As if Zoe couldn't hear, she hissed, "We said we weren't going to talk about that!"

"Aw, babe, I was just thinking that if she gives that map to the sheriff, then the police will have it all the sooner."

"Actually, the state police are conducting this end of the investigation," Zoe said, ignoring the slur about the nature of her relationship with Ethan. "Ethan McKenna heads the county police."

The last thing she wanted was to put Ethan in the uncomfortable position of passing on evidence that had already been handled by someone who knew better. She did not think that the map had the least bit of relevance to Patrick Rourke's murder or Susan Rourke's disappearance, especially after she and Laurel had checked everything out, but the investigation would have been cleaner without their hands all over it. If at all possible, she wanted to leave Ethan out of that part of it.

"It's no problem," Laurel said. "I'll just tell her we found it, and if she wants to know, it's okay to tell her how we set off the traps, isn't it?"

"Sure. Tell her the truth. We want to find out what's happened to your sister."

"And who the hero is who killed Patrick Rourke," Dorsey let a slow smile take possession of his lips.

"You sound as if you knew him well."

"You ever meet him?" At the answering shake of Zoe's head, Dorsey continued, "Well, you'd know that you didn't have to know him for long to not like him. He loved making people hurt, and animals, too. Made the testosterone flow, I guess. Nothing against him, but just about everyone in these mountains can sleep easier now knowing he's not walking the hills with his guns. One time—did Laurel ever tell you this?—he was shooting at what he says was a bear and damn near put a hole through both of us! You see that hole in the deck over there? That was his damn bullet!

Some high-powered rifle he was using! He was way down below us. I think he fired on us deliberately, but I had no way of proving it."

"What do you think happened to Susan?"

"I don't like to say this in front of Laurel, but she knows what I think. I think she's dead. I think he killed her shortly after he took her. And I think he probably killed himself. I know, the police are saying she did it. But if she did, then where is she? No, what I think happened is that he was drunk, just like always, and he tossed that gun across the campsite. But you know how weird your reflexes can get when you're drunk. So, he tossed it, not realizing it was ready to go off. It hit the ground, fired, and killed him. Hoist, on his own petard. Don't you just love that expression?"

Laurel softly explained, "Dorsey went to college. He's even thinking about going to graduate school."

"First we're going to get Laurel through college. Then I'll think about grad school."

"Did you go to college?" she asked Zoe, although she was addressing her fidgeting hands.

A nod was not good enough when Laurel wasn't looking. "Yes. And some graduate school, too." College had been Cornell and Stanford, both on full scholarships, and then a graduate fellowship at Georgetown.

Laurel sighed. "You know, people think I'm rich, but I could never afford to go to college. Heck, Ruth and Ardell, they don't pay any rent to speak of. It's barely changed since they took over the Ordinary. They take care of their own repairs, but when they tell me about it, it's like they always expect me to offer to pay for it. And when they expanded and opened that lunch counter? I didn't raise their rent, even though I think they're probably making a lot more money now. And I know they raised the rates on the motel. I didn't even ask for more then. All I really have coming in is the rent on a couple of small shops in Sinksville and the rent on the dry cleaner's. And I work at the dry cleaner's part-time, just to save paying someone else!"

"But you've got all this land. Would your Grandpa Franklin begrudge you a college education?"

Dorsey snorted, and Laurel shook her head. "I've had offers. The last guys wanted to open a—What was that, Dorsey?"

"A recreational community!"

"Yeah, right across the valley over toward Sinksville! Like this is a place where people from Washington, D.C., would come on the weekends and in the summer and build their little houses and pretend they lived in the country."

Dorsey showed his teeth, small, sharp, and white, a decidedly feral look. "They offered a ton of money."

Laurel nodded. "But Grandpap Franklin, he said that all developers ever brought was bulldozers and people. And that would be the end of the bears and the trout and the eagles. We've got 'em all out here, you know. So Susan and I never did sell. Not a single parcel."

"Do you think that might change, now that Patrick's gone and maybe Susan is, too?" Zoe asked. Once more, the land loomed large as a potential motive for murder.

"Are you kidding? After hearing the same thing from Grandpap all the time? We're not selling, are we, Dorsey? Susan's got to have a place to come to, once this is all settled. And we like it here just fine."

"What about college?" Zoe prodded. "Selling even a piece of land, maybe one that you can't even see from here, would likely finance your education."

Laurel shook her head as if Zoe were too thick to understand. "If I had to do that to go to college, I wouldn't go. Dorsey and I have been talking about Berea. It's all work-study. It wouldn't cost me that much. Or maybe I'll do some kind of correspondence courses. The main reason I haven't gone up 'til now is I haven't wanted to leave here. I'm still not sure I do."

Dorsey nodded. "Whatever you decide, babe."

"What did you study, Dorsey?" Zoe asked.

"Me? Boozing and gagging, mostly. I've got a degree in English, though. How about you?"

"Criminal justice and cultural anthropology undergrad." She had designed the major herself. Her graduation thesis had examined the relationship between criminal activity and those who enforced the law. It was more than corruption on police forces that she studied. It was a closed culture of support for criminal behavior. Her graduate studies focused on law and law enforcement. She had always planned to work for the government, not as a defender of the way things were, but as a proponent of Justice. Capital "J." Despite her experiences in D.C., her goals were unchanged, and her basic idealism remained. Given her family history, she figured she had inherited it at a genetic level.

"Hey, equally useless! Not bad! I've been telling Laurel she could probably even get credit for some courses so she wouldn't have to take them. She reads all the time. She's just about gone through the entire library in Russell Creek."

The object of his short speech blushed and twisted. "Dorsey!"

"Hey, don't be afraid to let people know you've got a brain and you know how to use it! You're always figuring things out. Sometimes I like to brag about you. Heck, you know she's the one who designed this deck. She's the one who read up on it. She even figured out blueprints, which look to me like some lunatic got loose with a ruler. I helped with the heavy work, but the rest is all Laurel's. Her Grandpap Franklin would've been real proud to see this."

She flashed him a look of unadulterated joy, and then hid it under her hair. In a small voice, she said, "I deliberately didn't put a railing on that end. People thought it wasn't finished yet, but it was. I left it open because I thought maybe Patrick might stumble off it some time when he was drunk. That's what I was hoping, with all my heart. So then Susan could be the way she used to be, and not be worrying all the time about saying or doing something wrong. I didn't want to push him off or anything. I just wanted him to take one step too close to the edge. I guess now I could put up a railing and some chicken wire, and then we could finally let the dogs out here." She nodded to herself and asked Dorsey, "Don't you think they'd like to be out here with us sometimes?"

Early the next morning, Jill Simone called to let Zoe know they were planning to operate on her cat. She hurried through the morning rituals with the current members of her feline family. Before she left home, Ethan called, and although she knew there was a lot she wanted to discuss with him, all Zoe could do was blurt out that the red cat was going to lose his leg.

By the time she pulled up at the veterinary clinic, the sheriff's car was already there, and Ethan was waiting beside it. Zoe's stomach was jumping, but she could not refuse the coffee he offered.

"It's ridiculous," she said, blinking back tears.

After a couple of sips, Ethan relieved her of the coffee, fortified himself with a swig, and slid the cup onto the hood of his car. He slipped an arm around her shoulders as they rang the bell at the back of the clinic. Silently, he offered her his folded bandanna. He was the only man she knew who still carried anything remotely similar to a handkerchief.

The door opened, and Jill herself let them in. Ethan nodded to her.

"He's still in his cage. You can go visit if you want."

As she and Ethan started toward the bank of cages, Zoe said, "I think I'm going to call him Hot Fudge. Will you change his records, Jill?"

"Sure."

"Hot Fudge?" Ethan asked.

"Who's not going to love him?" Zoe smiled.

The cat lay in the back of his cage, his ears flat, his injured left paw stretched out in front of him.

Jill came up behind them. "The gangrene's going to kill him if we leave him any longer. He seems strong enough for surgery now, and I can't justify waiting any longer. He'll be okay with three legs. You'll see. My sister in Baltimore has a three-legged cat, and she runs so well that most people don't even notice she's missing a limb. Now this guy will lose a front paw, so it'll be a little harder on him, but he'll have full use of his back legs, so he'll still be able to jump on your counters, Zoe."

Ethan laughed. "She'd put up a ladder for him if he couldn't."

"Hey, I heard on the radio this morning that another woman had gone missing. They said they're questioning her husband. What do you know about that, Sheriff?"

Ethan shook his head. "That was in Elkins. Outside my jurisdiction. Women leave their husbands every day. Just because someone in a nearby county left hers and it made the news, I'd hardly say that case is related to Susan Rourke's disappearance."

"Maybe," Jill conceded, "but don't you think it's strange that she just disappeared?"

"It's not illegal to leave a relationship," Ethan shrugged.

Jill nodded skeptically and put a strong hand on both their shoulders. "Say your goodbyes. Hot Fudge is going to get ready for surgery now. You can call after noon to find out how he's doing."

Before they parted, Zoe invited Ethan over for dinner later. By then, they would know the outcome of the surgery, and the atmosphere and the time would be more conducive to conversation.

In the meantime, Zoe figured work, or something close to it, would help her pass the long morning to come, so she headed out on the road toward Sinksville. The trees were gloriously bright against the blue sky, with each leaf straining like a Miss America contestant in a bathing suit to show off its stuff.

She rolled down the window and let in the cool air. Along with it came the scents of damp earth, downed leaves already beginning to decay, and just a hint of winter.

She pulled in at the Ordinary and went inside. Ardell greeted her from the lunch counter, where a few people were finishing their breakfasts, and Ruth nodded as she sipped at a mug of tea or coffee from behind the main counter. Zoe sauntered over toward her, deliberately concentrating on the day, and not on the cat who was probably staked out on the operating table by now.

She pulled a copy of the *Russell Creek Bulletin* from the top of the pile and set it in the middle of the counter. "Do you have a map of the trails around here?"

Ruth put down her mug, fished at a stray strand of hair tickling her neck, and pinned it up as she said, "Only foot map we carry is the Pioneer Trail. You thinking of taking a hike today?"

"Well, I was thinking of taking the path from here to Laurel Taylor's place. She mentioned that it used to be the only way to reach her house."

Ruth pursed her lips and sighed. "I don't know if all of that path exists anymore. Trees blow down, bushes grow up, and before you know it, the path is gone. Do you know we've got volunteers who come every month or so and clear their sections of the Pioneer Trail?"

Ruth raised the mug to her mouth again. "Once people stop using a trail, it tends to get overgrown mighty fast. Are you thinking Susan is somewhere up there?"

"I don't know. But it's a place she'd know, and maybe, if she's there . . ." Zoe shrugged.

"She would have been found already if she were up there. Besides, like I said, the trail isn't marked at all. You'd lose your way in no time."

"But didn't you say you picked berries on top of one of the mountains on the way there? Couldn't you draw me a map?"

Ruth smiled as she shook her head again. "Zoe, I couldn't even draw you a stick figure. It wouldn't be anything you'd recognize."

"How about Ardell, then?"

"Ardell? She don't go out walking those old trails anymore." She raised her voice. "Ardell? Do you remember the way over to the Taylor place? By foot? Could you draw this young woman a map?"

Zoe smiled. She hadn't been called a young woman in quite some time.

Ardell finished wiping off a table and then used the same towel on her hands as she left the lunch counter. Her sister still wore a shawl over her clothes, but Ardell sported a knitted wool vest and tan pants with creases so crisp they could have snapped.

"It's been a long time since I've been up in those hills," Ardell shook her head. "I'm not sure I could find my way anymore."

"All I need is a point in the right direction," Zoe appealed to Ruth. "Draw me as crude a map as you'd like. I've got a compass. And I know up from down."

Ruth frowned. "Why don't you just let it be? If Susan is hiding up there, she'll come out when she's good and ready."

"What if she's hurt?" Zoe could not get the image of Hot Fudge out of her mind. Behind it lurked the blood-spattered sidewalk where Karen lay.

Ruth shared a look with her sister. "I'll tell you what," she said. "There's still fruit on some of the trees in an old orchard up there. I'll take you that far, and you can help me pick the last of the apples and pears—whatever's left on the trees. How are you at climbing trees?"

Zoe had not climbed trees since she was a kid. "Just fine."

"Good. I don't know why the best fruit seems to stick on the tree. I'll point out what I want, and you can get it for me. Best to get it off the tree before that first hard frost gets here, anyway. There'll still be plenty for the deer and such to eat. Let me finish up a few things here, and then I'll get us a couple of baskets."

While Zoe waited, she bought a cup of coffee and read the paper. Willa had written the story about the missing woman from Elkins. "Three days earlier," Willa wrote, "Ora Lee Otis took the car to run to the grocery store for a few things and never returned. Her husband, Craig Otis, told reporters that he thought maybe she had been kidnapped by aliens, since it seemed as if she had vanished from the Earth. Her car has not yet been located. Police are investigating."

As Zoe read, Ardell came and looked over her shoulder. "Do you think he knocked her around?"

"Who?"

She pointed with her chin as she refilled Zoe's cup. "That woman. Maybe she finally had enough. Or maybe he finally killed her and hid the body."

"That's the way it happens all too often, isn't it?"

"Humph. Have you ever been in that situation, Zoe?"

"You mean, has a man ever abused me? No, not like that. Has it happened to you, Ardell?"

She set the pot on the table and slid into a chair across from Zoe's, nodding her head.

"My husband," she whispered. "He was like that. Even now, I'll hear a door slam or a certain pitch of voice, and I'll feel my stomach knot up."

"What happened? How did you manage to get away?"

"Ruth came and brought me home. It's more than fifty years ago now." Tears threatened, and she blinked furiously to keep them from falling. "You know the worst part? I loved him. I really did. I thought he'd get better. When he was sorry, he always promised to try harder. But then he forgot about what he'd said the next time he lit into me."

"The worst of it," Ruth said softly, having approached the table without either of them noticing, "is that he would have killed her eventually. I remember a time he broke her arm in two places. And it happens to women all over the country, every day. People don't understand how a woman can love a man like that."

She reached out a strong, veined hand and covered her sister's. "But it's easy, isn't it, Ardell? He beats you down, even if he never lays a fist on you, until you feel like you're lower than a scared dog's belly, and he cuts you off from your family and your friends. He took Ardell all the way to Huntington, so she had no one but him."

"With Patrick treating Susan the way he did," Zoe said, "it must have brought it all back for you." She could feel a lump in her own throat.

Ardell shook her head as a tear rolled down her face. "I shouldn't have told you this . . ."

At the same time, Ruth patted her sister's hand and said, "It's okay. You did leave him behind."

"He said he would kill me if I left him," Ardell said softly.

"What he meant was that it would kill him," Ruth said vehemently. "Why do men depend on women for so much? They claim they're the put-upon ones, but who ends up paying if things don't go well for them?"

"All men aren't that way." Zoe said.

Ruth studied her. "I saw you with the county sheriff at the Ramp Festival, didn't I?" Zoe smiled at her delicate phrasing. "Does he ever raise a hand to you?"

Zoe usually disclosed no details of her private life, but she had no trouble saying, "Oh, no, Ethan isn't like that, and neither is our relationship. We're cousins. Nothing more."

"Cousins," Ruth sniffed, as if unwilling to believe the statement.

Zoe nodded. "First cousins via my dad and his mom."

Ardell blew her nose. "Well, why don't you go finish those chores, Ruth, so you can show this young woman that orchard?"

"Yellow birch," Zoe said, rolling the small twig in her mouth and tasting again the crisp wintergreen on her tongue. She remembered the sweet tang from Moody Hollow, when her own Gran had stripped the bark from a piece of yellow birch for her.

Ruth nodded. "I always have to have a piece when I come up here. And since I only come up here in the fall, to me the taste means that it's time for picking fruit."

They had stopped by a stream to catch their breath and admire the view. They stood in a long valley, probably at the only approximately level ground between the two giants that rose in rolling mounds behind and before them. It was not a spot Zoe would have thought to stop for the scenery, her tendency being for wide vistas and windswept mountaintops. But here the trees were brilliantly colored, still lush and leafy, and the sun touched bright tendrils on the forest floor.

Ruth was nodding. "Most folks say they like spring, but I'll take the fall anytime." She breathed deeply. "There's a cleanliness to the air. I don't know what it is exactly, but it makes me feel like running."

"I know what you mean."

"I'd wager that you can run a sight better than I can. There was a time I could have matched you, though."

"Have you always lived around here, Ruth?"

Her gray hair was straying from its bun, but Ruth no longer took notice of it. Her face was weathered and wrinkled, chiseled and beautiful. No facelift could do justice to the fierce character that was illuminated from within. Zoe hoped to look half as craggy and appealing when she reached Ruth's age.

"Always. I grew up on the other side of Sinksville. My daddy worked for the Taylors, and we farmed a patch of our own land. It was tough then, but we had what we needed." She shook her head and gave a little laugh. "Probably everyone around here worked for Franklin Taylor."

They began walking again. Ruth meandered in and out of the trees, along no discernible path.

Looking back over her shoulder, Ruth continued, "I take it you've been up to the house on the hill. It hardly looks like they're rich, huh?"

"Rich in land, Laurel said."

Ruth nodded. "It's been a good relationship. Ardell and I helped them grow up, and now they're helping us. I've got no complaints."

"Did Susan or Laurel ever talk to you about developing this land?"

"Building on it, you mean? Oh, no! Both of them are proud of the Taylor holdings. A few years back, Patrick Rourke wanted to open some kind of hunting camp for rich people. I think he had visions of flying the plane these people would be flocking in on and entertaining them at dinner every night. But Susan told him Laurel would never agree to the plan. I think it was easier for Susan to blame Laurel than to tell Patrick she wouldn't go along with his ideas. No, Susan and Laurel both love this land. It was the one sure thing old Franklin Taylor planted deep."

"If you were going to hide in these hills, where would you go?"

Ruth paused and briefly touched the younger woman's arm. "Zoe, honey, in a few weeks these trees are going to be bare. A plane flying overhead would spot a tent or a trailer. It looks like a big wilderness, but there's really nowhere to hide. I think Susan's dead. I think that husband of hers tracked her down and killed her. I don't know why Susan ever wanted to marry him. She was always running off to be with him. Ardell and I tried not to be too hard on her, but maybe we drove her away, drove her toward him."

She paused while she held a low branch out of the way so Zoe could catch it and pass.

"I hope to heaven that we didn't send her into his arms," Ruth continued. "But you know the way teenagers are. They always want to do what you're set against them doing. By that time their daddy was pretty much wasting away, and there was nothing he could do. He'd be drunk before the sun was up. That cancer was eating away at him, and he said there was no way he was leaving that mountain. So he just left Susan and Laurel to Ardell and me. Eventually, Susan got tired of listening to us and moved back home. And Laurel soon followed. I know their daddy didn't care for that Rourke either, but Susan knew how to work her daddy around."

Picking burrs from her sleeve, Zoe asked, "What do you know about Dorsey?"

"That one who just about lives with Laurel? He's a hippie."

"A hippie?" Zoe smiled. "I haven't heard that word for a long time."

"Well, that's what he is. His grandma lived just down the mountain from the Taylors. His momma and daddy left for

Detroit or thereabouts, even before he was born, as I recall, and no one expected to see any of them again. But a couple of summers ago, there he is, camping out in his grandma's overgrown garden, saying he's going to rebuild the house."

"Is Dorsey his first name or his last?"

She scratched her head, and they began walking again. "I don't believe I even know."

"Did he rebuild the house?"

"Nope. I think when winter hit, he found out just how bad roughing it could be. Next thing you know, he's moved in with Laurel. That girl's got such a big heart, she'd take in any stray. And that's what Dorsey was at the time."

"They seem to get along well."

"I ain't saying I think he's bad for her. I'm just saying I think she could do better. I don't think he mistreats her or anything like that. She seems happy enough." She gave it a moment or two, before asking, as if second-guessing herself, "Did it seem that way to you?"

"Very much so."

Ruth nodded, relieved. "You want them to do well, even though they're not really your own. I never married, never had children. Ardell, she never had children, either, so Susan and Laurel are like our own. We both think of them as part of our family."

As Ruth turned to go back to the path only she could see, Zoe tried again. "So you two know Susan better than anyone, maybe even better than Laurel does. Surely you've talked about it with Ardell. If Susan were running, where would she go?"

Slowly, she shook her head. "I swear you're worse than a dog with a bone. You just won't let go."

"How can you?"

"I put my trust in the Lord and in reality. I truly believe that Susan is dead. Those police officers, they said there was no trace of

Susan in that truck. No fingerprints. To me, that says she was dead when he left that trailer. Maybe he bundled her up in a blanket or something and stuck her in the back of his pickup. Then he could have dumped her anywhere between there and here. Or maybe even someplace else. That Patrick wasn't very smart, but he was sly. I think some hunter will find her body come a few weeks from now."

"But what if she got away from him? What if she's hurt somewhere, needing help that she can't get?"

"You can't think that way, Zoe. You make yourself crazy doing that. Me, I prefer to deal with what I know."

Zoe knew the dangers of getting emotionally involved. She had been dwelling on Karen and Paul almost as much as she had been thinking of Susan and Patrick. Her feelings about Karen's murder still registered high, not quite three years after her friend's death. She still felt as if she had led Karen into a trap and made it easy for Paul to gun her down.

And she still believed that she should have known what Paul would do. She had vividly known the kind of man he was. But she had been so excited to have Karen back in her life, to return to those days full of promise when they had been roommates in college, that she had not thought through or acknowledged that Paul would know exactly where to look for Karen. She should have known. Zoe had been selfish with Karen. And Karen was dead because of it.

"Zoe?" Ruth smiled indulgently at the other woman. "You went away."

Zoe nodded. "Just a side trip."

"Care to talk about it?"

"No, it's nothing."

"Ardell and me, we visit that new hospital over in Russell Creek sometimes. We go with our church group once or twice a month. Sometimes we see women there who've had terrible things done to them by their husbands or boyfriends. Yet, most of them don't want to say a bad word against those men. Some people in our group, they think those women get what they deserve. I think that's a hell of a thing, pardon my French, for those people to say. Those women are the ones we should feel sorriest for. They don't like being hurt. They don't like being cursed. But they know how much those men depend on them. And that's what ropes them in."

"You understand it very well, Ruth."

The older woman pointed with her chin toward a nearby orchard of stunted apple trees, sufficiently bowed and bent to look like bonsai out of control. "I've studied on it quite a lot. Me, I'd rather have no man. Too damn much trouble. But a lot of women don't feel that way. I just try to understand them."

As they entered the old orchard, redolent of cider and rot, Zoe continued to look around for signs of Susan's presence. Every squashed apple was examined for footprints, every bent twig for a piece of torn clothing. But she found no trace, no trace at all.

With baskets full, they started back at the same quick pace they had maintained on their way to the orchard, and did not take a break until finding the stream with its ferns and stumps. For the first time beginning to show her age, Ruth rested on a rock by the creek, closing her eyes as she leaned against a tree trunk behind her.

Zoe followed the water for a ways, thinking of the swollen stream she had crossed earlier in the week. She let her mind wander and found her eyes searching for caves along the stream or near the boulders that had been cast about like dice.

One bush a few feet from the water had turned a brilliant yellow, but something fiery among its lower branches caught the sun and winked at her. Going closer to investigate, she found a man's ring, with a red stone set in gold.

It was not until Zoe attempted to pry the ring from the bush's tendril-like branches that she realized the thing was still attached, by the thinnest of sinew, to a small bone. At the base of the bush lay more tiny bones, some gray, some reddish, all of them weathered and worn.

She could see no trace of the bones that had once comprised the rest of the skeleton, but it felt to her as if she had stumbled onto the remains of that popular campfire ghost story that ends with a hook dangling from a car door. Her phantom had hold of only a bush, but its grip on the button that produced goose bumps was just as strong.

Her teeth involuntarily hit against each other a few times as she stood and pointed. "Ruth, look here!"

Ethan smiled tiredly as he removed his jacket. His face was streaked with dirt, and his jacket and shirt mud-spattered. Before stepping into Zoe's house, he removed his boots, which were near unrecognizable with their heavy layering of muck. His day had been spent tramping through the hills while Zoe waited at the police station, where she had been taken to give her statement.

"Don't worry about the mud, Ethan," she told him. Then, seeing that his smile only grew broader, she demanded, "What?"

He shook his head, but the smile would not wipe off. "I was just thinking that it was probably the first time someone had asked to use the phone so they could call their veterinarian."

"Well, I had to see how the little guy was doing. It's not every day someone gets a leg amputated and comes out of it okay, you know."

Still grinning, Ethan took off his holstered gun and locked it in the built-in cabinet in what was now the dining room. One of the things that endeared him to Zoe was the way he always locked his gun away when he was in her house. It was only the two of them and the cats, but he took care anyway.

Zoe had stopped carrying a gun when she gave up working in D.C. It was a personal choice, not a necessity. She knew she would have no trouble getting a permit to carry one. But she wanted nothing to do with guns anymore. And, without pushing the point, Ethan had silently let her know he understood.

"Well, they were still talking about it when I got back there," Ethan chuckled as he stooped to greet the shy black cat, Caramel. "You'll probably be written up in their newsletter, under 'Strange Requests.'"

"I'd probably still be there in a cell under 'Strange Suspects' if you hadn't admitted to knowing me."

"I'm still wondering what made me open my mouth." He conspicuously laid his briefcase on the dining room table, popped the locks, yawned, and stretched. "Okay if I grab a quick shower? I didn't even stop at home."

"Of course. You know where everything is. Dinner'll be ready when you come down."

He looked to his briefcase before meeting her eyes. "Maybe dinner could wait a minute or two."

"Maybe so."

As he bounded up the steps with renewed energy, Zoe propped up the lid of his briefcase and had a look inside.

She pulled out the report on top. It was a more detailed account of what had been found around Patrick Rourke's body and in his truck. As she began reading, she reached for a chair and sat down. Cherry Pie, a sweet brown tabby, stretched himself out on top of the paper, and Zoe simply rolled him from side to side while she read.

The officer in charge had searched several routes from the truck to the site where the body had been found, and no trace of a container for the moonshine had been discovered. The conclusion was that Rourke had gotten the moonshine from someone, probably in the hours just before he had died, since the level of alcohol in his blood was high. So far, though, the police had no idea who that someone might be, nor whether he or she had played a part in Rourke's murder.

The preliminary report from the medical examiner stated that the official time of death was estimated to be at least twenty-four hours before the body was found and might easily have been earlier.

It was also still unclear exactly when Susan had been taken. The premise the police were going on was that she had been snatched the first day Patrick had not shown up for work.

There still existed the remote possibility that Susan Rourke was lying dead or severely incapacitated somewhere in the woods and that someone else had killed Patrick. That explanation would better satisfy the question of why fingerprints had been wiped from every available surface, including shotgun and truck cab. And why the body had been moved after death. But so far no one was speculating concerning just who that murderer might be.

Zoe went back to the preliminary autopsy report. No traces of rope or rope burns had been found on Patrick Rourke's wrists or ankles. The knuckles of his right hand were severely abraded, as if he'd been in a fight. Fresh bruises and scrapes were apparent on the rest of his body. No scuff marks marred the heels of his boots. If his body had been dragged by one person, it had not been dragged far.

The report confirmed that he had been killed by a single blast, the majority of pellets concentrated through the heart, shot from several feet away. His blood alcohol level was high enough for impairment but probably not high enough to make a practiced drinker black out. The results of further blood tests and chemical analyses were pending.

There were no traces of Susan's hair found on Patrick Rourke, no drops of her blood, no smears of makeup or lipstick.

Zoe grabbed the next batch of stapled sheets in the stack. It was a report of the search of Susan's trailer. There, too, except for the window pane, no traces of blood were found, although there was extensive evidence that a knife had been used. The pillow, bedsheets, and mattress had been raked with the same sharp blade, and some pictures and walls had been similarly attacked. Plates and cups had been smashed.

The blood on the window was not a match with Patrick's. So far, no one seemed to know what blood type Susan was, although the logical conclusion pointed to it being hers. Her fingerprints were smeared in the blood. They matched fingerprints found in her car, around the trailer, and in the house she had shared with Patrick Rourke.

Zoe felt water dripping down her neck as Ethan leaned over her, parting her hair, tickling her skin. "Ethan James McKenna!" Zoe warned exaggeratedly, deliberately imitating his mother.

Turning to face him, she saw that he had changed into an old pair of jeans and a sweatshirt he had left at the house after helping her with some outside painting.

Ethan held up his hands in surrender and said, "I'll start dinner. You keep doing whatever you're doing."

But the next sheaf of papers was about a robbery at the Russell Creek mall. She had reached the end of the reports about Susan and Patrick Rourke.

Zoe stood and stretched. Cherry Pie got one more chuck under the chin before she headed for the kitchen.

Ethan stood at the cutting board. "So?" he asked. "Find any answers?"

"Mostly more questions. Are there any conclusions about those bits of bone I found today?"

He was cutting up onions and peppers, and the raw smells drifted around the kitchen. Ethan shook his head. "The medical examiner says they're most likely years old, and it wouldn't surprise him if they were decades old. Not days or weeks, at any rate. They probably belong to some farmer. The best guess is there's an old graveyard somewhere nearby. Whenever it rains heavily, that creek and its tributaries rise and flood. It could be that flood we had last spring washed out the bones. As far as we could determine, there are no unsolved homicides in the area. Aside from Patrick Rourke, of course."

Zoe dumped the last of the season's green beans into the sink and began washing and sorting. "These hills are dotted with graveyards. I think I even found one on the George place. It makes me wonder if there isn't one on this property."

"I wouldn't be surprised. Lots of families had their own cemeteries. I guess that's where all the ghost stories originate. After all, people are sharing their everyday living spaces with the dead."

"What about that ring? Do you think you'll be able to use it to identify the bones? It was a man's ring, wasn't it?"

"Sure looked that way. But it had no inscription on it. Nothing that would identify where it came from. Just a big old red stone in the middle of it. Besides which, it must be decades old. Who knows what kind of records jewelry stores kept back when it was made. Unless some local family can describe it, I'd say the ring and its owner will remain unidentified."

"Just like that? Case closed?"

"More like case never opened."

After dinner and chocolate were behind them, Zoe and Ethan had grown drowsy discussing Laurel and Dorsey. It was Dorsey who stuck in Zoe's mind, Dorsey who hid some secret. If going after the owner of the ring currently offered no leads, Dorsey still sat tight on top of that land near Sinksville.

"I'm going to look into Mr. Dorsey Dorsey," Zoe decided. "Why can't he have a first and last name like everyone else?"

"Like Cher? Roseanne? The Artist Formerly Known as Prince?" Ethan yawned, grimacing as he examined what was left in the bottom of his coffee cup.

"Yeah. Exactly. I'm going to find out where he's from and what he's doing here. And what he's hiding. I know it's something. I only hope it's Susan Rourke, alive and well."

The next morning, Zoe decided to begin with the vehicles in Laurel Taylor's small parking area. She had noticed they were both registered in West Virginia, but there had been no reason to note their license plate numbers. If one or the other were registered to Dorsey, she would have everything: his full name and permanent address.

The drive from Beverage was more of a challenge than usual, with dense fog settled like cotton wool in more spots than not, an alien invasion that had landed overnight. Winding and full of switchbacks, the road was not the easiest to drive in the best of circumstances. The fog made it almost impossible. Zoe crept along, hunched over the wheel as if a few inches closer to the windshield would make a difference. Brake lights were as likely to rear up at her as mountainsides. She took her time while considering turning around and going back to Russell Creek, the county seat, for county tax records. There, she could eventually, somewhere in the haphazard filing, find out who owned the land behind Laurel's.

But county records were not yet computerized. Without knowing the exact designation of the land, it might take her all day, or longer, to figure out who Dorsey was. If one of the vehicles was registered to him, though, she would have him right away.

She had not stopped in Russell Creek that morning, although she had spoken with Jill Simone about picking up Hot Fudge later in the day. The veterinarian had not yet determined whether she was ready to release the cat.

Slowly, Zoe inched along. She had reached the point where she did not want to miss the turnoff that led to Laurel's driveway. Everything looked changed, bled of color in the monochromatic mist. Huge boulders loomed menacingly at the side of the road, and trees seemed to lurch at odd angles, as if they had been mysteriously suspended while caught in the act of falling.

After finding the turnoff, she drove up the graveled drive, and the stones beneath the car tires crunched loudly and unnaturally. She reached the parking area, turned in, and parked beside the

Saturn. The sudden quiet as the engine died seemed just as out of place as the noisy gravel had been.

Stiffly, she got out of the car, flexing her joints, trying to ease the tension from her body. She crouched behind the Saturn and wrote down its number. Then she moved to the rusty pickup and got that one. Looming out of the fog and parked beside the pickup was a car she had not seen before. It was a station wagon. The make and model had either been removed or had rusted off, so she could not know for sure anything about its vintage or its lineage, but it was huge and boatlike; rust and primer blotted out whatever color it might once have been. She copied down the number of that dinosaur as well, noting that it displayed a "Russell Creek University" student parking sticker on the back bumper.

She did not intend to stay around any longer than the time it took her to put away the notebook, but she heard disembodied voices in the fog.

"He'll be fine," a male voice said. "Don't worry. We'll make sure he's well taken care of. They all will be."

"Laurel would be devastated if something happened." Zoe thought she recognized Dorsey's voice.

"Well, don't worry. We'll be back next week. When did we say? Thursday?"

"Yeah, Thursday, at the latest," a woman said. "The money will be all straight by then."

They were getting closer to Zoe, and she was stuck. True, she was surrounded by fog, but she could melt into it a lot easier than her car could. It was an old, nondescript Chevy that blended well in a crowd but tended to stand out on its own.

The tramp of feet on the path was louder. Any minute now, she knew she would be visible. Guiltily, she shoved the notebook in her pocket. If she followed her gut and ran, started the car, and hightailed it out of there, not only were they likely to know that they had been overheard, but there was also a good chance they would be close enough by then to see her car, if not identify her as well. Running would get her nowhere.

As walking figures blurred into view, still half-obscured by the fog, Zoe dashed back to her car. By the time they saw her, she had opened the door and was groping on the floor of the driver's side for a pen that was already in her fist. Muttering to herself, she glanced up, and she hoped, was surprised to see three people staring at her. She smiled and waved as she straightened, closing the car door behind her.

Dorsey's face was not as open and trusting as it had been before. To be honest, Zoe thought, neither would hers have been had she found an uninvited visitor in her driveway. Dorsey hustled the couple to their car while they talked in low, agitated voices. They both wore blue jeans and sweaters. Her top had a flowery pattern woven into it in contrasting colors; his was a plain knit. Her hair was spiky short and very black, with matching lips and nails. His hair was longer, curlier, and more windblown, although it was the same dark shade as hers. He scuffed a hiking boot in the dust.

"Hey," Zoe said, cocking her head, "don't I know you from the university?"

"I don't think so," the young woman said.

"Yeah, I was at the library the other day . . ." It could have been true. She often used their resources.

"I don't think so," the young man echoed.

Dorsey hurried them over to the car.

"Is Laurel up at the house?" Zoe asked Dorsey, sauntering toward the station wagon as if she had just noticed it. She wished she had managed a peek at the contents of the glove compartment. "There were one or two things that occurred to me that I thought I should ask her."

Dorsey fingered his sweater, deliberately avoiding looking at his companions. "Some cop was here yesterday evening. He just kept asking her the same questions over and over. I think she'd prefer to rest."

"I won't bother her, I promise. I'll just run on up to the house and be right back."

"She's not at the house," Dorsey said. "She's out."

"But her car is here."

He squared his shoulders. "She's out with her dogs. She does that when she needs to get away."

"Okay. I'll try her again sometime. Thanks. Sorry to bother you."

Zoe got into the car and slowly cranked the engine. She wished there was a way she could follow that station wagon without being seen on the lonely roads and without losing it in the fog. She comforted herself with the knowledge that as soon as she could get to a phone she would know who the cars were registered to. With any luck, the time that took would not affect Susan Rourke's fate.

"Hey!" Dorsey called as Zoe began to leave. "How much did you hear?"

She turned. Obviously, there had been a hurried conversation. "What do you mean?"

Dorsey took a deep breath, stole a hurried glance at his companions, and said, "We've got his dogs. His hunting dogs. We took them."

"Whose dogs?" Zoe asked.

"Patrick's. He was always mistreating them, forgetting to feed them, not exercising them. They're hounds. They've got to run. Laurel was sick about it. So last week, we went over to his house and took 'em while he was at work. We've got 'em hidden where no one will find them."

"What will Laurel be devastated about if something happens?"

He exchanged a look that said, "See?" with his companions.

"We're going to have the most aggressive male neutered next week," the woman said. "Our animal group is paying for it. Then we'll do the other two. If things work out, we might even be able to have them all done at once."

Dorsey explained, "I don't have the money for it. And without the neutering, those dogs will just keep running and fighting. And they're about driving Goodness and Mercy crazy. We can't keep the two groups together at all. Laurel and I didn't know who to turn to or what to do. Now, though, it'll all work out. The dogs'll be taken care of and, once all this dies down, Laurel and I will just move them up to the house. They'll be easier to care for and easier to find new homes for."

"Where are they now?"

"I told you, where no one will ever think of looking for them. But they're being well taken care of. Even if you want to tell someone about it, I don't think you'll be able to find them."

What if liberating the dogs had been provocation enough to start the killing? Suppose Patrick had come home in the middle of the snatch? And what if Susan had come by and gotten in the way?

Zoe said, "I'll need some assurance that Susan Rourke isn't hiding out with the dogs."

Dorsey shook his head. "Susan? No way. If we knew where Susan was, we'd tell her there's no reason to hide anymore. The wicked witch is dead!"

Zoe stopped at the parking area beside the Ordinary in Sinksville to make her calls. In order to keep it personal, she needed an outdoor phone, and this appeared to be the only one in town. Just to be certain of privacy, she checked that the adjacent bathrooms were empty.

Using her calling card, she soon found that both the Saturn

and the pickup were registered to Laurel Taylor. That information did nothing to shed any light on who Dorsey might be.

The station wagon belonged to Mary Ann Monroe, whose permanent address was in Parkersburg, all the way on the western side of the state.

The phone there was listed under Cecil Monroe, and the woman who answered, after hearing that Zoe was a friend of Mary Ann's who had lost touch, kindly informed her that her daughter was currently enrolled in Russell Creek University. She provided the phone number and the address of the house Mary Ann shared.

Taking a further chance, Zoe asked, "You wouldn't happen to know if Dorsey's still going to school there, too, would you?"

"I'm sorry, but I don't believe I know anyone by—You don't mean Tommy, do you?"

"Tommy?"

"Tommy Jeffries. He used to babysit Mary Ann and her little brother Seth, even though Tommy wasn't but two or three years older. He went to Russell Creek first. I think he wanted to get as far away from Parkersburg as possible, but his grades weren't good enough to get into one of the bigger schools. I believe his going away is what gave Mary Ann her interest in going there, too.

"Dorsey, you said, right? You know, he always said he was going to change his name. Even at thirteen or fourteen, he hated to be called Tommy. He thought it sounded babyish, although his daddy was always called that. It was over here at our house that he first heard big band music and Tommy Dorsey. My husband and I inherited a big bunch of old 78s, and we used to play them for the kids all the time. They'd make fun of them. I didn't think any of it had rubbed off!" She sounded pleased with herself. "So you've met Tommy, too?"

"Last summer, through this animal group we all belong to. He seemed very nice, but I only knew him as Dorsey."

"He's always been very nice. It's good that Mary Ann's keeping in touch with someone from home."

"Could you give me his parents' number? Maybe they'll be able to tell me how to reach him. I'm trying to organize a benefit, and I thought his help would really come in handy."

"Oh, I'm sorry, but his parents divorced and moved away several years ago. I really have no idea how to get in touch with either one of them."

"That's okay. Maybe Mary Ann can tell me. Thanks so much for the information."

"You're very welcome. When Mary Ann calls, I'll be sure to tell her you asked for her. What did you say your name was—?"

"Oh, it's Joyce," Zoe said, using the name of a favorite author. "Joyce Porter. And thanks again, Ms. Monroe."

She wrote the name in her notebook: Tommy Jeffries. It wasn't much, but it seemed right. She would have to check him out, make sure Tommy and Dorsey were one and the same, but it did seem to fit.

And now she really did have to face the reality of paging through the county records in Russell Creek. Did Tommy Jeffries have grandparents who had lived on the property adjacent to Laurel Taylor's? And had his parents moved to Detroit, as Ruth Cook had thought, before returning to West Virginia to settle in Parkersburg? It was a possible fit, but not a likely one. If Tommy Jeffries and his parents had been as close to the Monroe family as it seemed, then Mary Ann's mother likely would have mentioned a relative of his in the area. It was useless to speculate now, and Zoe hadn't thought to ask.

Resignedly, she tucked the notebook and pen back into her pocket, turned from the phone, and headed into the Ordinary. This time, the smell that engulfed her was of apples gone bad. She crinkled her nose as her eyes adjusted to the dimmer light.

It was as if the fog had entered, too. Only the overhead lights were on, and Ruth and Ardell were conferring over a basket of apples.

"What happened?" Zoe asked.

Ardell's lipstick was practically chewed off. Her hair looked as if it had not been brushed since she had gotten out of bed. "Hello, Zoe," she said with a distracted frown. "I thought you might be the police."

"The police? What's happened?"

"We never should have rented him a room," Ruth said through clenched teeth. "I knew he was trouble when I looked at him. Didn't I tell you to say we were full up?"

Ardell snapped, "Well, any fool could see there were only two cars in the parking lot! And that nice young couple was waiting to check in right behind him. Was I supposed to tell him there was no vacancy and then offer them a room?"

"Who was it?" Zoe asked.

Ardell stamped her foot. "That Craig Otis! I wish I'd never set eyes on the man!" She wiped at her mouth before adding, "He's the one whose wife up and left him the other day. And it's no wonder! Did you hear the mouth on that man, Ruth?"

"That didn't happen in Bickle County," Zoe said. "What was he doing here?"

"He says his wife had one of our advertising brochures on the bed table!" Ruth exclaimed in exasperation. "Well, you know we have those things all over this part of the state, and they're even in the tourist centers on the interstates! What does he think, that we sent it to her and asked her to come on down?"

"What did he do?"

"He came waltzing in here a while ago, demanding to know where his wife was, and when we couldn't tell him a thing, he started to bust up the place! He grabbed two bottles of apple cider off the shelf and just poured one over that strip we use to plug all the lamps into. I turned everything off, just to be sure. I sure as heck don't want to start a fire in here. And the other bottle, he just raised it up and smashed it right over here. There are lots of pieces of glass in all the baskets. Don't touch anything."

"Don't you either, until the police get here," Zoe said. "Then I'll help you clean it up."

"You shouldn't have called the police, Ardell," Ruth admonished her sister. "It's going to make things worse."

"Where did he go when he left here?" Zoe asked. She had not seen anyone go through the parking lot.

"I don't know," Ardell shook her head. "I wasn't watching."

Ruth added, "You know, if he'd spent this much time worrying about that wife of his when she was home, she probably never would have left him!"

That got a faint smile out of Ardell. "How are we ever going to clean up this mess?"

"No one followed him when he left?" Zoe asked.

Ardell waved her hand vaguely. "Only Billy was here. He wanted to, but we wouldn't let him. He could get hurt!"

Zoe glanced across the mess. "Would you like me to go have a look around outside?"

Ruth lowered her voice and said, "You read about men shooting their wives and their girlfriends. He might have already killed his own wife! You don't know. We have no way of knowing if that man is carrying a gun! He could be out there just waiting for someone to try to follow him! No need to invite trouble. You just wait here, like the rest of us."

While she did as Ruth requested, Zoe said. "The other day, Ruth, you mentioned that Dorsey's grandmother had lived in a house behind Laurel Taylor's place. Do you happen to remember her name?"

Ruth looked at Ardell, and Ardell looked at Ruth. Both had cocked their heads, mouths poised on the verge of speech. Zoe could not see the family resemblance when they stood side by side, but in gestures and facial expression, they were mirror images of each other.

Ardell's laugh broke the pose. "Maybe it's just the excitement, but I can't put my finger on it."

"Wasn't it Gamp or Grump or something like that?" Ruth asked.

Ardell waved her hand as if brushing away a mosquito. "You're thinking of that movie! That Gump thing—" Zoe watched as Ardell's expression changed, and understanding washed over her features like a windshield wiper on muddied glass. Suddenly she could see again.

She tutted a finger at Zoe. "It was Woods!"

Ruth thumped her on the shoulder. "That's why I was thinking of that movie. I was thinking of Forrest. Yep, it's Woods. Or, maybe Wood. Anyway, it's one or the other. It must be more than twenty years since she died. I'm surprised we remembered that one!"

"I'm the one who remembered it," Ardell pointed out. "Why do you ask, Zoe?"

Zoe shook her head. "It's no big deal. I was just talking to a friend last night, and she said her family used to visit grandparents around here. From the way she described it, I thought that might be the place."

"What's the grandparents' name?" Ruth asked eagerly. "We've been here forever. We'll know the place."

"I wrote it down at home, but I left the paper beside my phone. I know it wasn't Woods. Maybe it was Jeffries?"

Once again, Ruth and Ardell silently communicated with each other. "Nope," Ardell said. "That one doesn't ring a bell. There's no one by that name around here. Never has been. We'd remember it."

"Eventually," Ruth said with an easier smile. "But, no, I'm

sure there's never been anyone by that name around Sinksville. Maybe over in Feller County."

"Maybe," Zoe conceded, only half concentrating on the elaboration of her lie. Her mind was already resignedly preparing to go through the county tax records. "She said she was just a little kid at the time, and it had been a long time ago. It's no big deal."

Cleanup wiped away the entire afternoon. Ardell and Ruth insisted on picking up each piece of glass from the area rug by hand, assiduously preventing Zoe from carrying out her plan of hauling the whole thing out back and giving it a good shaking. Ruth thought they would all likely get glass slivers in their eyes. So the sisters painstakingly lifted out each shard. Zoe was permitted only to wield the broom, and then the mop, across the scarred wooden floor.

It wasn't until the following morning that Zoe was able to get to the Bickle County records office in Russell Creek.

On her way, Zoe stopped at the vet's to visit with Hot Fudge, who had been kept overnight again, just to be sure. He was coming along, but very slowly. Stitches covered at least a third of his chest, so Zoe kept her eyes focused on his, which were huge, the pupils nearly covering the orange irises.

After making sure there were no outstanding warrants on Tommy Jeffries or Mary Ann Monroe, she headed for the records office, prepared to sift through years of paperwork. A student intern helped, and eventually she uncovered the information she wanted.

Isabel Woods had last paid taxes on her property twenty-six years earlier. After that, her daughter and son-in-law, both named Cortland, had inherited, and they had kept the property current for the next three years. Since then, there had been nothing. The property had not been sold for back taxes, but it was cited as derelict.

Zoe used the coordinates on the tax record to find the exact location of the property on the detailed county map, which covered an entire wall of the records room. No access road was marked, although there was a broken line that the legend labeled a path. Zoe wrote down directions, crudely copied the map, and set out again toward Sinksville.

Snooping was what Zoe had in mind, so she could hardly park at Laurel Taylor's house and hike over the mountain from there. She had to follow the county map, trying to distinguish what was blacktopped lane from what might be a long driveway or an unmarked road. Eventually, she came to the remains of an old schoolhouse, the end of the pavement. It was marked on her map with a bell.

The trees met overhead in a yellow canopy, but enough leaves had already fallen to carpet the lane and let in light. She pulled far off the road, although she had not met another vehicle in the two or three miles she had traveled on it, and parked right beside the schoolhouse.

Zoe had begun her formal education in a similar structure, but the ruins here looked like a foundation for a garage, and a small garage at that. Tile blocks formed the lower walls. The upper ones had been made of wooden boards, and what was left of most of those sprawled among the bushes and trees that competed inside the small space of the structure. On the part of one wall that still stood, traces of faded whitewash remained.

Zoe circled the little school three or four times before she discovered what looked to be no more than a deer track leading into the trees. It was all there was, though, so she followed it, checking over her shoulder every so often, noting landmarks for the way back.

The trail widened a bit, and Zoe felt more certain that she was on the right path. An abandoned mine was marked on her map, and she found evidence of one just about where it should be.

At last the way leveled out, and the walking became easier. What must have once been fields were demarcated with lines of piled stones, impediments that had long ago been removed so a straight furrow could be plowed.

A few viable apple and peach trees remained. There were some brambled tea roses and a couple of flowers Zoe recognized from seed catalogs, but she could not identify them. A birdhouse lunged at a crooked angle off an old, dying oak.

Eventually, in a small hollow in front of her, structures appeared. The barn there still stood, but Zoe thought she would not want to be near it when a wind came up. Through huge holes she could see trees on the other side. Rotted boards slumped against what remained of the walls, and orange-rusted nails glinted wickedly, like neon tetanus advertisements.

The house was built of native stone, and was not what she had pictured at all. It did lack a contiguous roof, but most of the windows were intact. Two-storied, it must once have been proud testament to native craftsmanship. Even now, abandoned, it was not humbled.

As she drew nearer, Zoe could hear hounds baying. She had figured this was where Patrick Rourke's dogs would be hidden. What she was not sure of was whether Susan would be with them.

Two doors were latched from the outside, with silvery hook and eye in one case, where the wood no longer fit against the jamb, and with a new sliding bolt in the other.

Zoe flipped the hook and stepped quickly inside, shutting the door behind her. The shock of seeing a stranger silenced the dogs for a moment, but then one blue hound began barking, and the other two quickly joined in.

She took a quick reconnaissance, fully aware that her retreat might have to occur hastily. The stairs to the second floor were boarded and secured with nails. There was no way a person could have gotten up there—at least not from this level. The dogs did have access to a low basement with a dirt floor, which they had made liberal use of when nature called. With the hounds alternately wagging their tails and barking apprehensively as they followed her from room to room, Zoe made a quick circuit of the house.

Food bowls were lined up on the floor of what must once have been the kitchen. The linoleum was black in places where the pattern had worn away. The bowls were mostly empty, but the water bowls were full, indicating that the dogs had already been seen to at least once that day.

As Zoe looked around, taking the time to make sure no one not canine was living there, the dogs began to lose their initial fear. They crowded around her legs, making walking difficult. She petted them as she waded through them, opening closets and cupboards.

After a second time through the house, her eardrums vibrated with the constant barking of the dogs, but she was satisfied that no human was currently in residence. There were blankets and pillows on the floor, but the evidence pointed to strictly canine usage.

As she left, Zoe quickly eased out the door to prevent the dogs from following her. They set to baying as soon as she replaced the hook in the eye. She listened for a moment without moving, shushing the dogs even though she knew it was futile. As she turned and looked up, she found her face level with, and nearly touching, Dorsey's.

His was red with anger, and his hands balled into fists that were already rising.

Zoe raised her hands and stepped back, colliding with the door. The hounds yowled even louder. It took her a few seconds longer to find her voice. "I promised I wouldn't tell, and I won't."

"You shouldn't have come here. Everything was fine until you showed up. Laurel kept saying you were all right, but Mary Ann warned me to watch you. You keep asking questions, asking questions. You're a cop, aren't you? Damn! Why did you have to come here?"

Slowly, she began edging away from the house and from him, keeping her hands in the air. "I'm not a cop. I came here because I had to make sure Susan wasn't here. It's nothing personal. I just had to know. That's all there is to it, Tommy."

She had tried out his given name. Shocked, he lowered his fists. His face looked suddenly pale.

"Yeah, I know your name, Tommy. And if anything happens to me, I've left a trail clearly pointing to you."

"Are you from the state? Or maybe the feds?"

Zoe didn't understand what he was asking. "The state?"

Enunciating each word with the force of anger, he asked, "Do you work for the state?"

"I told you, I'm a private investigator. I don't work for anybody right now. I'm looking for Laurel's sister, Susan. We're not enemies, Tommy." She began to lower her hands.

"Don't try anything!" he warned.

"Tommy," Zoe said in a tone that begged for reason to be restored. Just to be sure, though, she did halfway put her hands back in the air. If it came to a fight, she thought she could rely on her body to remember enough self-defense to get both of them out alive. The last thing she wanted to do, however, was escalate the possible level of violence. She would much prefer to defuse the situation she was already in.

"You're asking me to believe you don't know anything about what's going on here?" he demanded.

"I know you have Patrick's dogs hidden out in this house. I know the house is not yours or Laurel's. It never belonged to your grandmother. And I know Susan isn't here. I also know that you don't want to face an assault charge."

"I can't just let you walk away."

"Why not? Look, my car is right down that other way. How about we both go down there, and then I can drive you around to Laurel's house?"

"You'll go blab about the dogs," Dorsey said, biting his lip. His face was still pale, his hands opening and closing spasmodically.

"Is that why you killed Patrick, Tommy? So he wouldn't blab about the dogs?"

"I didn't kill Patrick, and you know it." The answer was a growl.

Zoe asked, "Come on, Tommy. Do you really expect me to believe you just stole Patrick's dogs, and he let you? You're not that stupid, Tommy, and neither am I."

"Don't call me that! My name's Dorsey. You got that?" He took a step toward her, and Zoe took an equal one in retreat. The cadence of the dogs' baying stepped up.

"I got that."

"Patrick wasn't there! I told you! You want to know how things were at Patrick's house? The dogs lived in cages in the backyard. Cages. Barely big enough to stand up and turn around in. Just plain wire on the floor. No bedding. None! And the nights are getting pretty cold. And he bred his bitch whenever she came into heat, never giving her a rest. Aren't you going to ask me why we didn't call the police on him?"

"No. I've seen what they call the animal shelter." It was a concrete block rectangle behind the the fire station in Russell Creek. There were no full-time employees. There was no humane officer or even a dog warden.

"Besides that, he wasn't even breaking any big laws! The dogs always had water. He fed them enough to get by, most of the time. They didn't have adequate shelter, but no one really seemed to care about that."

"You and Laurel cared." Zoe took a step away from Dorsey, and he seemed not to notice.

"Yeah. We did." He said it defiantly, proudly. "We planned it for a long time. Patrick was supposed to be at work when we took them. The house was dark. Susan was already gone. We didn't know that was the night he went missing. We only went to get the dogs."

"So you haven't told the police that you were over at his house."

"What difference would that make? No one saw us! Besides, Laurel was his sister-in-law. She had every right to visit. We had borrowed a van, and we backed that sucker right up to the end of the driveway. Used our wire cutters and let loose those dogs. It was the thrill of my life. You have never seen dogs so happy."

"But you've got three males. What happened to the female?"

"I don't know." His voice was sullen. "She wasn't there when we went for them."

"I think we should go talk with Laurel," Zoe suggested. "And then you two should tell the police what you've just told me."

"No!" Dorsey had been calming down, but suddenly the anger again threatened to overwhelm him.

"That path leading upward behind you, is that the one that goes to Laurel's house?"

Zoe strode purposefully toward the path without waiting for Dorsey's reply. It wasn't her first choice in terms of direction, but

Dorsey seemed determined to try to stop her from heading for her car.

He grabbed for her arm as she passed him, and she lunged sideways in order to avoid him.

Suddenly there was no path beneath her feet, and she was scrabbling for lost ground, trying to find a safe landfall before gravity chose one for her.

Pebbles and rocks joined the cascade around Zoe, and from far off, she heard Dorsey's voice but couldn't understand a word of whatever he might be saying. With a thud, she hit earth, knocking the wind from her lungs. After that, it was enough to hold on.

More pebbles rained down on her, then stopped.

Nearby, full of concern, Dorsey asked, "Are you okay? Can you move?"

Zoe sat up. There was a stitch in her side, but breathing was already beginning to be something she didn't have to concentrate on anymore.

"I'm fine," she said at last, waving off his hand even though she made no move to crawl back up the steep, but relatively short, slope.

When she had regrouped sufficiently, Zoe gazed calmly upward and saw Laurel and her two dogs staring back.

"We heard the commotion," Laurel explained. "Are you all right?"

Zoe nodded again. "Watch out for that first step there," she croaked.

"There is no first step there, Zoe."

Dorsey stood up beside Laurel. He wiped his hands on his jeans.

"She found the hounds," Dorsey said. "We've got to decide what to do."

"I guess we'd better talk, then," Laurel said, as she reached down a hand to help Zoe up.

"It's on account of he loves me," Laurel said shyly, catching Dorsey's eye. "It makes him do crazy things. Are you sure you're okay?"

"I'm fine," Zoe assured her, gingerly testing a scraped elbow.

"She knows where the dogs are," Dorsey said to Laurel. "We'll have to move them."

"She's not going to tell, are you, Zoe?" Laurel asked.

"I already told him that."

They reached the house from the path that ran in front of it, the path Zoe had almost kept following when she had first come to see Laurel. All of them piled inside, dogs and people, one somewhat the worse for wear.

They ended up in the kitchen. Laurel put a pot on the stove for her famous instant hot chocolate. She turned to Zoe and said, "Could I ask you to go back to that little room with the couch, just through there? I want to talk to Dorsey for a minute."

Zoe finished her first glass of water, took a wet towel to clean her face and hands, and walked slowly toward that small doorway, stealing glances over her shoulder.

Once Zoe stepped inside the room, Laurel pulled shut a pocket door behind her. Zoe figured Laurel and Dorsey must have moved out of the kitchen then because she couldn't hear a thing, even with her ear to the door.

She turned from the door and waved to the dogs, both lounging on their couch. Neither made a move toward her. One gave a happy bark, and both began to thump their tails.

Zoe headed straight for the ladder, back to what she was calling the lookout room, the one with the windows that faced the mountains and Sinksville, far in the distance.

There, she sank down on the floor, legs stretched out in front of her, and made liberal use of the wet towel. All around her, clouds drifted through gray sky.

Turning her head slightly, Zoe spied the display case that had gotten her up to the room to begin with. Why, she wondered, had Laurel's grandfather ever dragged the thing all the way here from the Ordinary? It must have meant quite a lot to him.

With an involuntary groan, she shuffled closer to the glass. She took her time inspecting the fossils and the arrowheads, trying to imagine a time when this area had been unexplored frontier to the Europeans pushing their way west.

Serendipitously, a glint caught her eye. Hidden in the back corner, under an eagle feather, was something red.

She felt a bruise brewing on her left hip. Telling herself that the glimpse of red could not be what she thought it was, she went behind the case and slid open the door. Reaching in, she lifted the feather and revealed a man's garnet ring.

As she leaned over the display case, the ring between thumb and forefinger, Zoe studied it inside and out. Like the one that had been found on the bush, there was no inscription, no school or class year engraved.

"This is it," Zoe whispered almost in awe, and hooked the ring over her thumb so she could safely descend the ladder with it.

When she looked up, she saw Dorsey's head protruding through the hole in the floor.

"Oh, geez," he said, "now she's stealing stuff."

Laurel was right behind him. Both backed down to let Zoe join them.

"Laurel," Zoe asked, displaying her find, "where did this come from?"

Laurel's eyes widened, and she shrugged. "I have no idea. It was my grandpap's. My dad never wore it."

"What does it signify? Where was it bought?"

"I really don't know." She held out her hand for it and said, "Let's go into the kitchen. The hot chocolate's ready. We have some things to discuss."

"I'd like to hold onto this, just for a little while. There's another one I found that looks like an exact match. This one could help identify who owned that other one. Would you let me borrow it?"

"Sure, as long as you return it."

"I will." Zoe slid the ring into the watch pocket of her jeans, where it was not likely to get lost.

The little table in the kitchen had not been meant to seat three, but they made do. After each had a mug, and cookies had made the rounds, Laurel placed her hands flat on the table. Her nails were bitten to the quick.

"Dorsey and I are going to tell you everything," she said. "We're trusting you not to tell."

He began to say something, but a look from her shut him up.

Laurel continued, "Those dogs are worth a lot of money. I'm going on the assumption that you didn't know that."

"I didn't. How much are they worth?"

"Lots. Thousands apiece. That's why Patrick trapped. So he could afford the dogs. Hunting dogs are worth a lot of money to a lot of folks, and Patrick had some of the best. His dad's the one with the reputation. People paid him to let their dogs mate with his. Patrick, he didn't love the dogs or anything. He just took care of them because they'd bring him money."

Dorsey put his hand over Laurel's. "Those dogs were not living dog lives. They were living like concubines or prostitutes. Can you understand that?"

"She gets it, Dorsey. Anyway, so we had to take them. We spent a lot of time planning it. We got some help from some friends of Dorsey's, and we set it all up. We figured that once we got them neutered, he wouldn't want them anymore. We were planning to pay him eventually, over time, and if necessary, we were going to give him a small piece of land. He could trap on it or do whatever he wanted. It would've been a fair deal. And we thought we could keep the dogs up here, if they'd be okay, and if not, Dorsey's friends would help us find them good homes. That's all there was to it. No one ever meant for it to get out of hand. When you came by, Dorsey was only trying to protect what he knows I care about. We just couldn't keep the dogs here with the police coming and going. It was too much to try to explain."

Earnestly, Dorsey said, "If you tell, who knows what'll happen to those dogs."

"She won't tell, Dorsey. She already told us that." Her eyes didn't leave Zoe's. "That's what you said, isn't it, Zoe?"

"That's what I said."

Laurel leaned into Dorsey, deliberately butting him with her shoulder. "I told you how she found that cat and rescued him from Patrick's trap. And I told you how we went around and took care of the rest of the traps. I believe her, Dorsey. I do. Now, apologize to her, so there'll be no hard feelings."

The last time Zoe had seen them interact, she would have sworn that Dorsey took the lead in the relationship, that Laurel was too shy to voice her side and relied on him to do it for her.

But now Zoe saw a different facet. In a crisis, Laurel was the one who kept her head. He relied on her.

Dorsey swallowed audibly. At a look and a dip of the head from Laurel, he said, "I'm sorry, Zoe."

"There's one more thing we have to get clear, though," Zoe said. "Your name."

"There's no need for you to know that," Laurel said quickly.

Morosely, Dorsey said, "She already does."

Laurel smiled at her, one-third wonder, one-third puzzlement, and the rest fear, which stretched the corners of her mouth down and back. "How'd you do that?"

"It doesn't matter," Zoe said. "What matters is that you're hiding, and if I could find out, so could anyone else. If you don't want to come clean to me, that's your business. But it's probably only a matter of time before someone else starts looking into it, too." Zoe leaned forward on her sore elbows, "Did you have anything to do with Susan's disappearance?"

"No! I wish I did! And I'm not hiding a thing! Dorsey is the name I've gone by for years. No law says I can't use it."

"Unless you're using it for criminal purposes," Zoe could not resist pointing out.

On the drive back to her car, Zoe took the opportunity to question Laurel about her grandfather's friends. She wanted to know who had known him, who he had been close to, who might still be alive.

"Aunt Ruth and Aunt Ardell, of course," Laurel smiled at Zoe. "They knew him as well as anyone, I guess."

"Did he have any close friends?" Zoe asked. "Male friends?"

Laurel looked to Dorsey, who was driving, as if for inspiration, as she answered, "He had a bunch of friends. They'd hang out and get drunk together, from the stories I always heard. But I don't believe any of them are still alive. Maybe Orney Pickett is still around. He was in some old folks' home in Elkins, last I heard. I think his daughter lives around there. I don't know what her name might be. Uncle Orney, though, he was something else. He always told me he'd give me a nickel if I could snatch it out of his palm before his fingers closed. And he had a million stories about how things used to be. He was a nice one, always paid attention to Susan and me."

She turned again toward the backseat, her eyes wide. "I just realized he had one of those rings, too! I was just picturing his fingers closing over that nickel, and I saw the ring. I never really thought about it before! How about that?"

"There's no one from his family still around here?" Zoe wrote "Orney Pickett" in her notebook, making a wild final "t" when the car hit a pothole.

Laurel shook her head. "Not that I'd know of."

"Who else knew your grandfather?"

Dorsey briefly rested his right hand on the nape of Laurel's neck. He gave her an affectionate squeeze. His smile was anxious. Not for the first time, Zoe wondered what his terrible secret might be.

"That's all I can remember," Laurel pronounced.

"How about someone who might have done business with him? Someone who came calling on a regular basis?"

"Oh, there was Alma Eskew, but you probably don't want to know about her."

"Why not?"

"She was never really a friend of my granddad's. She tried to get him to marry her once or twice. She was always trying to get someone to marry her. The men used to make fun of her, although I didn't understand what it was all about when I was a little girl. Whenever she used to come into the Ordinary, Aunt Ruth would tell me that Alma had tried to steal Aunt Ardell's husband before she married him. Aunt Ardell said Alma tried too hard."

"Is she still around?"

"Oh, yeah. She's more of an age with Aunt Ruth and Aunt Ardell. Maybe even younger. It's funny, but I've always thought of her as old. She lives out on Old Mill Road, along the Pioneer Trail, a mile or two from the Ordinary. You can tell her house. It's the one with the swan flag out front. It's real pretty."

"Laurel, is there a graveyard on your land? Maybe somewhere someone who was a close friend of your grandfather's might be buried?"

Laurel slowly shook her head. "I never heard of one. My great grandpap's grandpap was one of the founders of the Resurrection Church, over by Feller County. He started the tradition of having the family plot in the cemetery there. As far as I know, there's no one buried anywhere else."

On the way home, Zoe followed the winding path of Old Mill Road and had no trouble finding the small house with the swan flag out front. But no one answered her knock.

She picked up Hot Fudge, all stitches and eyes, at the vet's, then spent some time at home settling him in his own room. To get him used to the sound of her voice, she carried in the phone from her bedroom and plugged it into the jack. She flipped open her notebook and dialed, first Sam Bennett, then Wyatt Harrison, and arranged to meet both men that evening.

The bar was called Portsiders, a barn of a building just across the Bickle County line. A jukebox with the volume in the red zone serenaded her inside. Some couples were out on the small dance floor, their feet crunching peanut shells as they all followed each other in a line dance.

Zoe let her glance wander around the darkened room. Wood and haze were the dominant decor. The floors and walls were finished planks, with knotholes for ornaments. Small electric lights fashioned to simulate candles stood shrouded in cigarette smoke on the glossy finish of the tables. None of the lights were bright enough for Zoe to test her wood identification skills.

Tables were round and of various sizes. Most were not yet taken, although the seats at the bar were almost gone. Zoe had deliberately arrived early, and as far as she could tell, before either Wyatt or Sam.

She snagged a table, ordered three beers, and pulled out a book on hunting dogs she'd borrowed from a deputy sheriff, closing her eyes slightly against the irritation of the smoke. The music switched to a bluegrass tune, and three couples who had been at one table together got up to show off their clog dancing skills.

As Sam Bennett and Wyatt Harrison sauntered in, their camouflage jackets blending in with others on the dance floor, Zoe waved them over. Just as they sat, glancing uncomfortably at each other as if regretting the agreement to meet her, the beers arrived. Wyatt ordered tortilla chips with cheese, and he and Sam spent a couple of minutes checking out the women in the place.

Zoe set herself squarely in the chair, elbows on the table, and said, "You two said you'd gone hunting and trapping with Patrick Rourke."

With a wide-eyed survey of the surrounding tables, Sam Bennett leaned closer to her. Someone had lowered the volume of the music, so he kept his voice low. As it was, she barely heard him say, "If you're trying to get more dirt on Patrick Rourke, you're not going to find it from us. If you're wearing a wire or something, and you want us to tell you he hunted and trapped out of season, we're not telling you a thing." He glanced around the room again before settling back in front of his beer.

She shook her head. "No wire, no recording devices, not even a notebook, guys. I'm not with the police. Like I said, I only want information. I'm not looking to sell it to anyone or to use it in any way against Patrick Rourke's reputation or memory."

Wyatt Harrison drank half his beer before wiping his mouth on the back of his hand. He growled, "You have to promise you won't use anything we say against us, either. You know, in case we might have done some hunting out of season or something. I'm not saying either one of us has."

"You want me to write it down?"

"Just say it."

"I promise I won't use anything you say about hunting or trapping out of season against either of you."

They exchanged a glance. At last Sam nodded, and they each drank, as if to seal the agreement. Wyatt finished his beer, and Zoe caught the server's eye and held up two fingers.

"You both trapped with Patrick Rourke?" Zoe asked.

They nodded. Sam's fingers drew acute angles in the condensation on the table. Wyatt casually cracked open a couple of peanut shells.

"Do you know if he had a system for checking his traps? Did he check the same one first every time?"

Sam shrugged. "I would guess so, although I'm not sure. Are you, Wyatt?" At the brief shake of the bigger man's head, he continued, "I know he had a map he used. He'd draw a new one every time he moved his traps. So I guess he had a system he followed."

The drinks and chips arrived, and the two men dug in.

"Do you know how often he'd check his traps?"

Around a mouthful of chips and beer, Wyatt said, "Every day. Usually twice a day, unless we started work real early. He was always bragging that he checked his traps more often than he had to."

"Well," Sam added solemnly, "I think he was worried that someone might find his traps when they were set where they shouldn't be, so he wanted to be the first to find anything in them."

"Some pelts are worth a lot of money," Wyatt said helpfully.

Sam nodded.

Wyatt's voice grew defiant. "I do know that if he couldn't check the traps, he didn't set them. Like, if he knew he'd be gone for a couple of days, he didn't set them until he came back again. That's the way he was."

"You're certain?"

Wyatt nodded. "Yeah. That way, if he got delayed or something, he wouldn't have to worry about somebody else finding them and maybe stealing from him. O' course, he'd have a hard time checking a trap when he was dead, wouldn't he?"

"If Patrick went on a drunk," Zoe asked, "would he still have set the traps?"

Wyatt gave a short laugh that turned into a choking cough. Sam smacked him on the back, and Wyatt grabbed Zoe's beer, which she had been carefully nursing, and downed it. He slowly shook his head. "I've never planned a drunk. You, Sam?"

He looked tentative. "On my anniversary I did. Last year."

Zoe ground her teeth. She tried another tack. "When you hunted with Patrick Rourke, did you each bring your own dogs?"

Wyatt answered, "Mine got the damn parvo year before last. I never had but a couple anyway. But Sam's got a few, and Patrick sometimes had his dad's running with his own, if he happened to be in his dad's good graces that day. Why? You figuring on using those hounds to find Patrick's killer?"

"I'm just trying to understand what happened," Zoe said. "Did Patrick do much breeding?"

Wyatt nudged Sam with his elbow. "Weren't you two going to cook up a sweet deal with your bitch?"

"Fell through," Sam said, taking a drink. "No way I was letting his hounds near her. And his dad had something else going. We never did work it out."

Zoe asked, "What was the matter with Patrick's dogs?"

"Weren't worth nothing," Sam said. "He run the breed into

the ground. At one time, there wasn't a better line of hunters than those hounds. Patrick took care of that, though."

Wyatt gave a snort of a laugh and said, "Hey, you think maybe it was one of the dogs that shot him?"

It was time to leave. Zoe knew she'd get no more from the men. They must have stopped for a few drinks before they met her. Given their condition, she knew it was a long shot, but she asked anyway, "If I wanted to buy moonshine, where would I go?"

Wyatt grinned. "You'd start by not calling it moonshine. Call it white mule. Otherwise, ain't no one going to sell you nothing."

"Yeah," Sam agreed, "white mule. It's like white lightning, but with a real kick!"

"But selling moonshine is illegal," Wyatt added solemnly. "Ain't it, Sam?"

"So if I were Patrick Rourke, where would I go to get white mule?" Zoe asked.

"Probably old Patrick brewed it himself, probably had a doubler right there in his basement. Or maybe out in those kennels behind his house. Maybe his hounds brewed it for him. Right, Sam?"

"Huh?" the other man blinked back the alcohol from his eyes. "Yeah, right, Wyatt. Right."

Aside from acquainting Hot Fudge with the sound of her voice, the previous night's work had proven largely fruitless. Zoe had tried calling Alma Eskew several times, but there had been no answer.

She hadn't had much more luck in her attempt to find the owner of the ring. When she checked the phone book, there were three nursing homes in the Elkins area. At the second one, she learned that Orney Pickett had lived there once but had died several years earlier. His daughter still lived in the area, and Zoe quickly dialed her number.

The woman remembered her father's ring at once. She had no idea what it signified, but she said the family had followed his instructions and buried it with him.

"I take it he wasn't buried around Sinksville," Zoe had said, raising her tone just a bit at the end.

"No, in Elkins. On a hillside, just like where he'd always wanted to live."

The following morning found Zoe again in front of the house with the swan flag out front.

"I hope I didn't wake you," Zoe apologized to the woman who peeked out of the crack of her opened front door.

She was shorter than average, her face tanned and strong. Eyes far apart under thick, arched brows; a nose that was probably called upturned in her youth; and a mouth poised to smile, or as quickly, close up, were just visible on the other side of the door. Disheveled auburn hair escaped from under the hand she had raised. She looked much younger than Ruth and Ardell.

"That's okay. It's time I was getting up anyway. Are you hiking the trail? Would you like a cold drink?"

"No, thanks very much, though. You're Alma Eskew?"

Puzzled, the woman nodded but did not open the door any wider.

"My name is Zoe Kergulin. I'm a private investigator, and I wonder if I could ask you a few questions. I'm trying to find information about a ring."

"Do you have some kind of identification?" Most people seemed to take Zoe's word for it. It felt like old times to pull out her ID. After closely examining the document, the woman handed it back and opened the door for Zoe to enter.

"I watch a lot of movies," Alma Eskew announced both proudly and as a warning. "I know not to trust strangers."

"That's generally a good policy these days."

"When hikers come to the door, I bring a drink out to them. It's not my nature not to trust people, but with my own eyes I've seen what can happen. Did you ever see *The Desperate Hours?* It was a brutal movie, just brutal."

The house was small and probably very cozy for one person. It looked as if there were three rooms on the ground floor, probably one or two bedrooms and a bath above. Alma Eskew showed Zoe to a love seat in the living room and pulled open the drapes at the rear of the room, exposing a picture window that looked out across an expanse of trees and down to a wide stream. Despite the gray day, the room brightened, illuminating built-in bookcases stuffed with videotapes. In between the bookcases stood a wide-screen television and, on a sturdy cart beneath it, a VCR. Both the love seat and the recliner, where Alma Eskew settled back, tucking her housecoat around her, faced the blank screen.

"I work at the video store, just up the road a couple of miles. At that new strip mall? It's open until the wee hours, and it's my turn for the late shift this week. That's why I kind of slept in this morning. I wanted to be up for the Gary Cooper movie they're showing on AMC this afternoon, though. It's one I don't want to miss. We don't have it at the video store."

"I have a thing for him myself," Zoe confided.

Alma leaned toward her, smiling. "Wasn't he handsome? And always so upstanding. I think Harrison Ford has some of his qualities, don't you? When I first moved in here, I thought I wouldn't be able to get along without cable, but I bought one of those little satellite dishes, and now I get more than I ever did on cable. What a wonderful invention! Do you have cable where you live?"

Zoe shook her head. She lived too far out.

"You should get a dish," Alma pronounced. "Don't tell me there's nothing you want to see on channels you can't get."

"'Mystery Science Theater,'" Zoe said with a smile. "I miss that one." One of her friends in D.C. still taped it for her intermittently.

"Get a dish. They're not those humongous things anymore. You can barely see mine."

"You should go into selling them. You're very convincing."

Alma Eskew cocked her head and smiled. "I hadn't thought of that. Maybe I will, next."

"Next?"

"I've discovered so many things in the last few years! Let me tell you, do what you like. Those are my words of advice for everyone. I waited until I was sixty to learn them. Thank goodness I didn't leave it until it was too late, though! Some people do. I've seen how bitter they get. I saw myself heading for the same cliff, and I didn't want to end up at the bottom of that. So, one day, I just said to myself, Alma, stop trying to do what you think other people expect of you. You're a grown woman. If you're not happy with your life, then fix it. But I'm not staying here with you if that's how you're going to be for the rest of your days. So I started to work at the video store. It's the best job in the world! But someday I'll have seen all the movies they have, and if the shine rubs off, well, then I'll just go and find something else. Who knows, maybe someday I'll come knocking on your door asking if you'd like to buy a satellite dish!"

"If you do, I'd have a hard time turning you down. I came to ask if you could tell me anything about this." Zoe fished in her pocket and pulled out the ring she had taken from Laurel Taylor's house.

Alma reached for it and studied it a moment, then walked over to the window with it, turning the ring so the stone gleamed. Her forehead wrinkled.

"It looks familiar, like I've seen it lots of times . . . Oh, I know. It was that poker club. There was a group of five men who used to get together at the Ordinary to play cards. I wanted to play, too, or at least to learn, but they wouldn't let me because I was a girl. In those days, we resented it, but we accepted it, too, if men said no girls were allowed."

Alma kept hold of the ring as she sank back into her chair. "The men in that group all got these rings. I don't remember why. Maybe it was just to show they were all in the same club. I do remember when they started flashing them around. They thought they were pretty special, I think. It was like they thought they were millionaires or something." She raised her eyes to meet Zoe's. Tears glistened there.

"Back then, I would have given anything to have been asked to wear one of these rings. I think I even took to wearing a locket under my dress, and I put a red stone in it. But that didn't really do the trick. Those men would be so cordial to me to my face, asking me to go get them more sandwiches and the like, which I was happy to do, and as I left, I'd hear them say nasty things about me. But I kept going back, just like a dog looking for a little pat on the head. I never did get it."

She ran her forefinger under each eye. "It took me so long to wise up. I know I was just a young girl then and didn't know much about the world, but I let those men treat me the way no one should have to be treated. They didn't beat me or, you know, hurt me the way some women get hurt, but they would use me like I was their servant and wouldn't mind being ordered around. And I didn't! Thank goodness I woke up in time!"

"Who were those men? Do you remember their names?" Zoe pulled out her notebook and balanced it on her knee.

"Of course I remember. There was Franklin Taylor. Well, he owned the Ordinary. Lord, but I had a crush on him. Now that I think on it, though, I have no idea why. He wasn't even good-looking. Nowhere near Gary Cooper! And there was Orney Pickett. He was a nice old man. And Jack Lamb. I was sweet on him, too, I guess. Now, he was handsome! He had that dark hair and dark eyes. I suppose I thought he looked like Tyrone Power. He married Ardell. She runs the Ordinary now, along with her sister, Ruth. And then there was Nolan Woods. I think he was a bit older than the others. He was already married, so I had no interest in him. And who was the fifth one? . . . It was Robert Rowder! I believe he moved to California shortly after that. I don't know what happened to him then. I never heard of him again. I'm amazed that I even remember his name!"

"So these card games took place before Ardell married Jack Lamb?"

Alma nodded. "I'd guess it was fifty years ago, or even more, now that I think on it."

"Do you remember how long they went on?"

"Not really. It probably wasn't more than two or three years. But I'll bet you it was three or four times a week. They'd set up a table as soon as the Ordinary closed. And the whole time the game went on, they'd be drinking the moonshine. Sometimes, folks came in to buy it, too. This was supposed to be a dry county, mind you, but you'd never know it by the way folks carried on back then."

"What happened after two or three years?"

"I'm not sure. Like I said, I was only allowed to hang onto the fringes of that group. I wasn't privy to the inner workings of those men."

"Are any of them still alive?"

Alma reached over and, almost wistfully, handed back the ring. "I'm not sure. Franklin Taylor is dead, of course. And Nolan Woods. He died in the army. Buried somewhere overseas, I believe, although Isabel fought long and hard to bring him back here. Maybe she got him eventually. I was never very friendly with her, so I really can't say what happened there. I think I read that Orney Pickett died a year or two ago. He had moved away already. I have no idea whether or not Robert's still preaching. That's what he used to do before he went to seek his fortune in California. That, and working for the railroad. The preaching was his calling, though. There was never any word about him in the local paper. And Jack Lamb? I don't know about him, either. I don't know where he went after he left here."

Zoe had Franklin Taylor's ring. Orney Pickett was buried near Elkins, presumably with his own ring. Robert Rowder and Jack Lamb had left the area. That meant the ring probably belonged to Nolan Woods, that his wife had managed to have him buried nearby. Zoe circled his name in her notebook.

"Do you remember when Jack Lamb left here?"

"Well, I remember the first time for sure. It was when he married Ardell. They moved to Charleston or Huntington, somewhere in that area. But Ardell wasn't happy, Ruth said, and she went to fetch her home. It wasn't too long after that when he showed up in a new car, just pining around, trying to win her back. I was still sweet on him then, and I tried to get his attention, but he only had eyes for Ardell. Eventually he got the message she was finished with the marriage, and he went on his way. I'll bet you he did well for himself. He was such a charming man."

"And when did Robert Rowder leave?"

"I don't remember if it was before or after Jack and Ardell married. Oh, it had to have been after because I believe he was at the wedding. Now that I think about it, I believe Robert did come back here once. For the Taylor family funeral. There was a terrible tragedy where Franklin's daughter-in-law and grandson drowned. After that, Franklin and his son, they became . . . " She groped for a word. "I don't know. It was like they were strangers to civilization after that. They both kind of gave up. Franklin, he tried for a while, but his son just dragged him down."

"His son wasn't part of that poker group?"

"Junior? Oh, no. He never did fit in with that crowd. He didn't like football or card-playing, spitting or wrestling . . . He never was one for the so-called manly arts."

"Are you saying he was a homosexual?"

"I don't know about that. I think he just had a different temperament. But Franklin always thought he was a sissy. Do you know the origin of that word? Sissy? It's sister! How about that! If you really want to insult a man, you call him a girl! I think Junior and his father just never did get along. I think those two old men hated each other. Junior was younger than me, but I think of him as being so old. I guess the cancer made him so shriveled and bent. Those two shared a house, but they never did get along. Those poor girls. It was so lucky for them when Ruth and Ardell took them in. Both men were too busy grieving and fighting to care much about raising two girls." She shook her head. "And then they died. One not too long after the other. Cancer took 'em both. Cancer and drink."

"So you know Susan and Laurel?"

"Their whole lives!"

"Have you seen Susan Rourke in the last few days?"

"Now, why would she come here?"

"Did she?"

"Of course not! You don't understand about my place in this town. Well, how could you, not having grown up here? I'm the black sheep of this place. I always have been. I never could fit in, no matter how hard I tried. And I tried pretty hard. Neither one of those girls would ever come here. I'd see them at the Ordinary, but they never set foot in this house, nor me in theirs.

"Did you happen to see that swan flag hanging out on the front porch? That's my emblem. That's me. I'm the ugly duckling who's turned into a swan. I don't care anymore if the rest of the town hasn't seen me flap my wings. I know in here"—she raised her fist to her chest—"what I am. I don't need them anymore."

"Where do you think Susan would go?"

Alma puckered her lips in thought. "I really don't know. Everyone I talk to seems to think she's lying out there dead somewhere. If I were her, I guess I would have gone straight to the police, if I could. Since she didn't do that, maybe she is dead."

"You said you've known her since she was a baby. Do you know where she used to play when she was a girl? Or when she lived with Ruth and Ardell? Did she have any friends she might look up?"

"Well, while those girls lived at the Ordinary, I believe they used to play on the Trail. The Pioneer Trail." She said it with some pride. "It crosses right over the back of my property. Most of us never did want the thing to go in, but we had no say in the end. Now, I don't mind it so much. I meet people who've come from far away just to see what the pioneers saw. Back when they were building it, I think every kid in town played there. You know, the men cut down trees and used these big machines to move the dirt around. Sometimes there was dynamiting, even. It must have been something for a child to see."

She shook her head, remembering. "It wasn't too shabby for a grownup, either. But, as I recall, the only person Susan used to hang out with was that Patrick Rourke. There were other girls around, but Susan always wanted to be with a boy." Alma sighed. "I hope she learned, before it was too late for her, too. I sure hope she learned."

Zoe deliberately put aside her pen. "If you wanted to buy moonshine, Alma, where would you go?"

Alma Eskew's face colored, and her hand covered her mouth as she smiled. "Now, nice girls never knew about such things."

"Sometimes they did; they just ignored the knowing."

Nodding, Alma admitted, "Maybe so. Back then, Franklin

was the one to see. He had a still—a doubler, he called it—somewhere right near that house of his. I don't know when he stopped making that moonshine, but he was famous for it. I remember he used to order quart jars by the truckload!" Her eyes misted with memory.

"How about if I wanted to buy some today?" Zoe's voice was low, but her body leaned forward, betraying the intensity of her interest.

Alma shook her head. "I wouldn't know where to begin to look. We're not a dry county anymore, so there's no need for it. But people still think homemade packs a bigger wallop."

She reached over and put a hand on Zoe's arm. "If you do happen to find out, though, would you let me know where I might buy a pint or two?"

"Who says the dead don't come back to life?" Zoe asked Ethan.

They had met for dinner at the only vegetarian restaurant in Russell Creek, near the university. He was not a vegetarian; she was.

"Zombies?" he asked with a smile. "Maybe you should have ordered something with more garlic."

He sipped from his beer, looking relaxed. The worry line that Zoe had seen so often lately between his dark eyes had disappeared for the time being.

"If there really were only five of those rings," Zoe said, "then whose did I find?"

"Who have you ruled out?"

"Orney Pickett, who is buried somewhere around Elkins, and Franklin Taylor. I have his ring in my pocket. I'm still trying to track down whether or not Nolan Woods is buried here or somewhere overseas. As far as I can tell, there are no members of his family still in the area. I've got a call in to the church at the end of the road in Sinksville. Maybe the pastor will know.

"I've spent a good part of the afternoon trying to track down Robert Rowder." Zoe began to play with her spoon. "So far, I haven't turned up a trace of him, and I've covered about half of California. You'd never guess how many Rowders there are, and not one of them has heard of Robert. I've got a request in for a search of driving license records for his name, but you know what kind of priority that's going to get.

"And Jack Lamb, another elusive character. He has no family left in the area, either, unless you want to count Ardell, who says she hasn't heard from him since the divorce, and good riddance to him, wherever he is." She abandoned the spoon and its clatter.

"You'll find out. You will. You'll narrow it down, and—" Ethan snapped his fingers. "The dead will rest in peace."

"Have you heard anything new?"

He shook his head. "Not a thing. I haven't even gotten a final copy of Patrick Rourke's autopsy report yet."

"There's still a warrant out for Susan?"

"Yeah. The longer it takes to find her, the worse my feeling about her gets."

"Me, too."

They were silent for a moment, contemplating unvoiced fears. Dinner arrived. Ethan immediately dipped into the chili, sans carne, while Zoe savored the stir-fried spicy vegetables with silken tofu that practically melted in her mouth.

"Did you have a chance to check out Patrick Rourke with the hunters around the station?" she asked.

Zoe had shared just about everything she knew with Ethan. She had told him about the dogs, about Dorsey, and about the animal group. In a murder investigation, she could ethically keep nothing back—although she had deliberately gone to Ethan with what she knew, and not to the state police.

She had sworn not to tell where the dogs were hidden, and she had not. Although she wasn't sure Ethan hadn't figured it out for himself. So far, he hadn't asked her to elaborate, allowing her to keep her promise to Dorsey and Laurel.

Ethan swallowed a mouthful of chili and nodded. "Graham Jenky and Nesto Hernandez both told me Patrick Rourke's dogs weren't worth what those kids claimed. Nesto remembered a case a couple of years ago."

Shifting so he could extract his notebook from the jacket that hung on his chair, Ethan said, as he began flipping through pages, "It's in here somewhere. Yeah, Patrick sold two pups to two different people. He'd had them advertised as Rourke's Kennel hounds. Apparently, that's his dad's outfit. Oldtimers around here claim that each breeder has hounds with different characteristics—some have better noses, some tree better, all the usual doggy stuff." He made a rolling motion with his hand.

"Anyway, his dad can just about name his price," Ethan continued. "He has a reputation for keeping up his lines, although Nesto says he's barely in the business anymore. But Patrick couldn't give his pups away. Folks claimed they didn't even look like hounds. Anyway, both people who thought they were buying Rourke's Kennel hounds took our friend Patrick to court, and he lost.

"According to Graham, Patrick's dad is the one who has all the skills. Patrick didn't spend the time or have the savvy. Those kids have inflated the dogs' worth, that's for sure. Maybe Patrick was trying to paint himself as a big man, or maybe those kids are just trying to enhance their own reputations. But, whichever, those dogs were not worth killing Patrick to steal. There's no hot market out there drooling over Patrick Rourke's hunting dogs."

With a flick of his wrist, he closed his notebook and laid it on the table. "Is that what you were looking to hear?"

"I wondered." Zoe pounced on the spoon again. "I sure wish I knew what Dorsey was hiding."

"His orchestra?"

"You're grinning."

"Hey," Ethan said, spreading his hands, "I'm enjoying the company, enjoying the beer, and the food's not bad. What else is there?"

"So for now," she said, "the dogs are okay where they are. Right?"

Ethan shrugged. "I talked to Ed West with the state police, and I mentioned that Patrick used to have dogs. He knew. There are kennels out behind Patrick's house. I don't think it's a lead the state cops are interested in following at this point. If those kids thought the dogs were worth big bucks, though, it is a possible motive for killing Patrick."

"Maybe, but it doesn't explain Susan's abduction." Zoe interlocked and raised her hands so they met under her chin. "Ethan, I'm thinking about asking my friend Beth in D.C. to see if she can find out if the Alcohol, Tobacco, and Firearms folks are interested in anyone in Sinksville. On the q.t., of course. I don't think they'd be interested, but it's a possible lead, and who knows . . . ?"

"Beth-at-the-FBI Beth?"

"That Beth."

He was shaking his head. "I wouldn't go getting messed up with them again. You'd be asking for trouble. And probably putting Beth right in the middle of it. Bickle County, too." That was his real dread. "Don't do it, Zo. That's my advice."

Zoe picked up her fork, avoiding his gaze. "Well, Beth wouldn't press it, and she was going out with that one guy for a while, that one who ended up as an instructor for them. Remember? I really want to find out about that moonshine that was found in Patrick Rourke's truck. White mule, Patrick's friends called it."

Ethan laughed. "That's the tradition of these hills. Remember my granddad's dandelion wine? That's what he called it, but it sure tasted like no wine I've ever had since. Anyway, in these hills, you're an outsider. And, as an outsider asking about it, you know no one's going to tell you a thing about white mule. Let that one go would be my—Geez, you already called Beth, didn't you?" He lowered his head into his hands in what was only partially mock exasperation.

"I had to, Ethan. She doesn't expect to be told anything, but she said she'd make some inquiries. If things get hot, she'll pull out. And if they turn their attention this way, she'll try to draw them off. She promised. That illicit liquor is the only lead right now that looks like it goes anywhere. It had to've come from somewhere. Someone who may have seen Susan or someone else in the truck with Patrick. Someone who may know a lot more than they're saying so far."

"That's a heck of a lot for some faceless, nameless person to know."

"Yeah. I realize that. But it's a lead that the state police don't seem to be following." Zoe raised her eyebrows. "Unless you know something different."

Ethan sucked at his teeth. "Hey, go for it. It's your call."

Zoe had never known a man who caved in so gracefully, a man who didn't argue when he knew he had no choice. "Ethan, did a will ever turn up? Either Susan's or Patrick's?"

"As far as we know, neither one had a will."

"So all that land reverts to Laurel? Or does part of it pass to Patrick Rourke's family?"

"As the grandfather's will was written, it passed from him to Laurel and Susan. There was a trust set up to protect it from being divided through marriage or divorce, although there are provisions for part of it to be sold, if the two women agree and meet certain specified conditions. Without the benefit of litigation and a court decision, though, I'd say it all goes back to Laurel. If Susan's dead."

"Too bad."

"Too bad?"

"Well, his family might have good reason not only to get Susan out of the way, but him, too, in order to grab the land. But if they don't benefit from his death, what good are they as suspects?"

At home, Zoe found the message light blinking on the answering machine. As she pressed the playback button, she realized the call was from Laurel Taylor.

Laurel said, "Dorsey and I have been thinking about how much you're doing for us, looking for Susan and all. We'd like to hire you, just to make it official. I know you said this was something you wanted to do, but we want it, too, and we don't see any reason why you shouldn't get paid for it. So please call and let us know what you charge. Thank you."

After the beep at the end of the message, Zoe still stood staring down at the machine. She shook her head, sighed, frowned. At last, addressing Chocolate Pudding, the oldest of her cats, who sat squinting up at her from next to the phone, she asked, "When was the last time someone offered to pay you for a job they could have gotten for free?"

Because of the spiderweb quality of the fog, Zoe had to pick her way carefully toward Sinksville, the road a sticky strand unseen before her, so she was later than she intended to be by the time she arrived at Laurel Taylor's house. When she knocked on the door, the dogs began barking.

Laurel peeked around the back of the house, from the deck that had no railing, and called out, "The door's open. Just come on through the house. Don't let the dogs out, though."

A short while later, Zoe joined Laurel on the deck.

Laurel had a fire going in an old, rust-colored charcoal barbecue. Her chair was pulled close to it. She gestured for Zoe to take the other seat, which was almost close enough to the fire to catch, should an errant spark glance that way. Laurel's cheeks were red, and her eyes flashed. A quilt with a familiar pattern was draped across her lap. Her gaze remained on the coals as Zoe pulled the plastic chair just an inch or two farther from the fire.

"You missed it," Laurel said with a grin. "Earlier today, the edge of the deck just disappeared. The fog was so thick, we were floating in the clouds. No view, no trees, no deck. Dorsey and I ate breakfast out here, and we were the last two people on earth. Almost!" She turned to face Zoe, and there was triumph plastered across her expression.

Zoe's eyes traveled down to where Laurel's hands were casually crossed across her midsection.

Zoe remembered that pregnancy test kit, abandoned on the piano, that she had seen the first time she had visited.

"I guess congratulations are in order, then," Zoe held out her hand and smiled.

If possible, Laurel's grin grew wider. "I have waited for this my whole life! I knew Dorsey was the one the minute I met him. The first night we slept together, I thought for sure I was pregnant."

She smiled sheepishly and shook her head. "I didn't know a heck of a lot back then. We weren't even married yet. Being with Dorsey, though, that's time that's gone so quickly. I keep waiting for the coach to turn back into a pumpkin. I think I must be the luckiest person alive."

They looked out over the valley, but all they could see was the edge of the deck and a vast ocean of fog.

Laurel said, "If Susan could be here to share this, then I'd really be in heaven. Dorsey wanted to stay home today, to celebrate, but his friends arranged to have all the dogs neutered this morning. They thought they'd speed it up because they have a lead on a family that's looking for a couple of hounds. They have lots of property to run on, and they're looking for pets, not hunting dogs. If they took two, that would be great! I don't want Goodness and Mercy to get all bent over it, you know. It's going to be bad enough getting them to understand that the baby's going to have to get more attention than they do. Right now, they think they're my babies." She drifted off into a beatific smile.

Suddenly, she turned to Zoe. "Do you have any kids?"

Zoe shook her head.

"Don't you want them?"

Zoe shook her head again. "Not really." She enjoyed her nieces and nephews, but loving them had elicited no evidence within herself of a strong maternal instinct. As far as she could tell, her biological clock had no alarm, and she quite liked it that way.

"Yeah," Laurel said, "I've heard that before. I never could understand it, though. Don't your arms just ache when you look at a baby?"

"Only if I hold one too long."

At length, Laurel turned from the contemplation of her belly to ask, "Well, did you bring the forms or the contract or whatever? We might as well get the business part over with."

Zoe sidled her chair just a smidge closer to the warmth. "Laurel, I don't feel comfortable taking you on as a client right now. If the offer had come at the beginning of this case, then maybe I would have considered it. But right now . . . Look, I knew Susan. Not well, and not as well as I would have liked to, but I did know her. That gives me a special interest in her to begin with. Also, I identify with what she went through, so that also prejudices my work. Third, I've seen you often enough that ours is something more than a working relationship, even if we don't call it a friendship yet. The point is, Laurel, that I can't take you on as a client. Not now."

"But I don't see why not. Why can't you? I want to pay you for the time you spend looking for Susan. It's what I'd want to be doing, if I could."

"Use your money for other things."

"But I know you could use it. I've seen that junker you drive. And look at your jacket. It must be years old. Your shoes aren't even leather!"

"It's a carefully cultivated look. In a few years, everyone will be dressing this way." Zoe pushed herself out of the chair and stood for a moment at the brazier, turning her hands this way and that, as if they were marshmallows toasting. "I'll still let you know if I find anything."

Laurel leaned forward. "But I need your services. And you're already on the case. Why won't you let me hire you?"

"For the reasons I just said, Laurel. It has nothing to do with you personally. Ethically, I just can't do it." Suddenly Zoe knew where she had seen that quilt before. It had been in the trailer, on the floor beside the slashed bedding. "Wasn't that Susan's quilt?"

Laurel stroked it, nodding. "It was my great-grandma's. Her sister made it as a wedding gift. The police told me I could have it back. I figured I'd just keep it until Susan can reclaim it." She beamed, "We were so lucky it wasn't damaged. This thing has been in my family for ages. Now, my baby's going to be able to use it, too."

In less than half an hour, Zoe was knocking on the door of the house adjacent to the church. The house was constructed of brick, an uncommon sight in Sinksville. It was a ranch, set on a level lot, far back from the circle that marked the end of the street. Flowers, looking only slightly careworn, still bloomed on either side of the walk, and the grass was weedless and well-groomed.

A woman who must have been about Zoe's age, in her mid-thirties, opened the door with a practiced, kind smile. Dressed like June Cleaver, in shirtwaist, heels, and pearls, her hair was short, dyed a uniform color, and sprayed in place. She looked Zoe over once and pointed to the right, toward the church. "The dinner will be over there, in the social hall in the back. But it's not for hours yet. Do you need a meal in the meantime, or perhaps some money to call home?"

Zoe did not deliberately dress down. She dressed casually. Or so she thought.

She pulled out her ID and flipped it open. "My name is Zoe

Kergulin. I'm a private investigator. I called yesterday and left a message about someone I'm trying to find. His name was Nolan Woods. He might have been buried from this church. Are you the pastor?"

Zoe ignored the woman's flustered look, which was quickly replaced by an efficient shake of the head.

The woman said, "That would be my husband. I'm the one who talked to you and took your message. I'm sorry my husband hasn't had a chance to get back to you yet. He's very busy with the dinner preparations over at the church. Perhaps he'll have a moment to talk to you, though. Would you like me to show you where he is?"

Nehemiah Charles was tall, rather burly, and overly cordial. A ready smile hovered around his lips as he directed parishioners in the setting up of long tables.

"Call me Nehi," he told Zoe. "Everyone does. We're getting ready for our weekly dinner here. Through three seasons, we provide an inexpensive dinner for hikers once a week. Some of them hang around for a day or two, just waiting for it. We're famous for it. We're even in the trail guidebook. And we regard it as part of our mission. We're not looking to convert anyone right off the bat. We just want to get them thinking about God.

"You wanted to know about Nolan and Isabel Woods, right? They were before my time, but I looked them up in our records. They were both members. Is that what you wanted to know?"

"I was interested in knowing where they were buried. I'm particularly interested in where Nolan Woods is buried."

"Is he some sort of relative?"

Zoe pulled the ring out of her pocket. "I found this last week in the woods not far from here. All I want to do is identify the owner and return it where it belongs. I know Nolan Woods had a ring just like this. If he was buried in the church cemetery, then I can eliminate him from my list of possible owners. If he was buried in a family plot in the woods, though, then I may be onto something."

"I see." His left hand shifted to explore his chin, as if he wore an invisible beard. "Well, I did pull out the cemetery file, and I did find both Isabel and Nolan in it. I'll show you where their plots are located if you'd like to see them."

The grass was overgrown in the small section of the cemetery, and it was shaded by a large sycamore that must have been planted many years before. The fog had dissipated enough so that the top of the tree was almost visible. Nolan and Isabel Woods shared a headstone, which revealed that he had preceded her in death by more than twenty years. Under the legend, "Father, Grandfather, Brother, and Friend," and running across the entire stone, were the words, "Deeply missed by their daughter."

Zoe had stood in their house, currently being used as a dog kennel, and she had seen the hand-hewn stones and rafters. She wondered where their daughter lived now and how often she thought of that house in the hills.

His hands clasped as if trapping a fly, Nehi solemnly stepped into position beside Zoe. He bowed his head, said a few words, of which Zoe caught only syllables, and they both turned away.

As they walked back toward the church, Zoe asked, "Would you please look up two other people for me? To see if you know where they're buried? Jack Lamb and Robert Rowder." She wrote the names on the back of one of her cards.

Upon leaving the minister, she walked back to the Ordinary, where she had parked. It was not yet eleven when she swung in through the front door of the Ordinary. Ruth, in jeans and a sweater, was waiting on a line of hikers. As she rang the register, she nodded to Zoe. Ardell bustled through the newer section, setting the tables up for lunch.

She was the one Zoe wanted to talk to.

"Hello, Zoe." Ardell flashed a quick smile and kept laying out napkins and forks, checking the salt, pepper, and ketchup supplies at the same time.

"We need to talk, Ardell."

She shook her head. "Not right now. After lunch. Billy overslept and is just getting the kitchen ready now, and our other counter help is late. If these tables aren't ready, lunch won't be served at all."

"Give me half of what you've got. I'll help. We can talk while we work."

Ardell accepted. Zoe ran to the kitchen, washed her hands, and quickly returned. She took a stack of napkins in the crook of her arm and a bunch of forks in her fist. In a few minutes, they were finished. Ardell wiped at her forehead with an extra napkin.

"This part of the place is so much work. I wonder if we didn't make a mistake in putting it in," she said. "What is it you wanted to ask me? Come, let's sit at the counter and take a break before the crowd comes in."

"Ardell, you know that Ruth and I found a small part of a skeleton the other day."

"Yes. I don't know when we've had such excitement around here."

"We also found a ring with a garnet stone. Ruth said she didn't recognize it, but I thought you might." Zoe pulled out Franklin Taylor's ring and held it toward Ardell. The older woman studied it briefly, not taking it from Zoe's hand, before she nodded.

"Yes, I believe I do recognize it. It looks like one that belonged to my husband."

"Could he have been buried in a family plot in the hills between here and Laurel's house?"

She was taken aback. "Without me knowing about it, you mean? I don't think so."

"Do you have any idea where he is now?"

"None at all, Zoe. I've never had the desire to know. I assume he married again and got on with his life."

"I heard that he followed you here, after you left him."

Her chin began to quiver, and she dabbed at her eyes with the napkin. "That's true, although I can't imagine who else around here would remember that. It was shortly after I came back to Sinksville. He showed up one day and acted like he was courting me all over again. I told him it was over, but it took him a few days to understand. Eventually, though, I guess he got the message because he told me goodbye and said he still loved me. He told me he'd write, or at least call, once in a while. I had no intentions of accepting a letter or a phone call, but if it made him feel better, I thought that would be fine. He left town then, and I never saw him again. I have no idea where he might be now."

"He never tried to get in touch with you after that?"

"Never. I guess he finally realized it was over between us. It couldn't have been easy for him. Divorce was almost unheard of back then. Especially in a small town like this. I thought it would be easier on him, in a big town like Huntington, than it was on me, here in little Sinksville, where everyone's in everyone else's back pocket."

"Do you remember the significance of the ring?"

"It had something to do with a school club and with poker. A bunch of these men used to get together every so often to play poker and gossip, you know the way men do. Well, someone made fun of them once, not one of them having more than an eighth-grade education. You couldn't blame them, you know, since that was as far as the school went. There was a little schoolhouse, way over on the other side of Franklin Taylor's land. All the grades were jumbled together inside. So these men all got to drinking and talking, and before you knew it, they were ordering rings out of some catalog. They called them their school rings. They were all real proud of those rings."

"Who were the others in the group?" Maybe there was a sixth player who had not yet been mentioned.

"Let me think. It's been quite a while. Let's see. Besides Jack, there was Franklin Taylor. If there was gambling going on, even penny-ante poker, you can bet old Franklin was involved. If I'm not mistaken, he's the one who organized the thing, probably corrupted all those younger men." She smiled to let Zoe know she was only kidding. "Orney Pickett. I'm pretty sure he was one. Tall and thin, just like you'd expect from hearing his name. Real handy, too. And I believe Nolan Woods was a part of that group. His family built that old school. There were one or two others who came and went, but they weren't part of the main group. I'm not sure I can recall who they were just now."

"Would any of them have given away their rings, or maybe sold them to someone else?"

"Are you kidding? Franklin Taylor used to say he'd auction off his wife before he'd give up that ring. They all thought they were something else when they wore those things, although I'm not sure just what. Hot stuff, I imagine." She shook her head, letting a small smile escape.

"Do you know what happened to those men? Are any of them still around?"

"Nolan Woods died long ago. In some kind of accident with the armed services, I believe. And Orney Pickett, he left to go live with his daughter around Elkins. In fact, I do believe I heard that he had died."

"Was Robert Rowder a part of that group?"

"Robert Rowder! Oh, I haven't thought about him for quite a

while." She lowered her voice. "He used to say to me, 'Ardell, how about we ditch Ruth tonight and take a stroll in the moonlight?' I was just a young girl, and I was so flattered that he noticed me. He wasn't from around here originally. He worked for the railroad, I think. I believe he was part of that group, now that you mention it. But I don't recall if he had the ring or not. I suppose he did, just to fit in with the others, if nothing else."

"Do you know what happened to him?"

She shook her head, her eyes straying to the kitchen to watch as Billy got busy, rattling pots and pans. "I guess the railroad sent him on to somewhere else. He was a preacher, too, although he was the unholiest man I ever did meet. He'd drink and cuss and gamble. But on Sundays, he'd gussy himself up, slick back his hair, which was a brilliant shade of reddish gold, and lay on the fire and brimstone. He talked about taking the Word on a touring show. Maybe that's what he did. My goodness, but these are people I haven't thought about for ages!"

"So you never heard about him after he left here?"

"Not a word."

"Do you remember anyone else who might have gotten a ring, too?"

"Robert Rowder! I'm going to have to ask Ruth if she remembers anything else about him. But, as far as the rings go, I don't believe there was anyone else who got one. I can't think of another person who might have been in that card club on a regular basis."

"Did you and Ruth run the Ordinary back then?"

"Goodness, no! It was all Franklin's operation. We helped him out, waiting on customers, stocking the shelves, and such, but we were much too young to run this place."

"How about his son, Laurel's father? Was he in on the games?"

Zoe caught a sheepish look on Ardell's face before she turned away. "Oh, no. Junior deliberately went the opposite way, just to defy Franklin, I think. He started drinking pretty early in his life. And Franklin was a tough one to stand up to, believe me. Ruth and I were quaking before him the whole time we worked for him."

Two people wandered over and sat at one of the tables. "Well, I'd better get busy helping Billy. I never should have taken a break now. We're going to be way behind." She scrambled behind the counter, grabbing a white apron to tie over her slacks.

"Thanks, Ardell." Zoe studied the ring again, turning it this way and that, before slipping it back into her pocket with a vexed frown.

By three in the afternoon, Zoe had covered about four miles of the Pioneer Trail and interviewed eight people. No one she talked to had seen anyone who did not appear to be a tourist, nor had anyone reported any break-ins, or had food stolen, or had clothing disappear from a line.

Zoe admitted she was at a dead end. It looked as if Susan Rourke had simply vanished from the face of the earth.

The trip back was a lot faster than the one out, since she was not stopping to ask questions. A drizzle began about two miles out of Sinksville, not far from Alma Eskew's house. Fog began darting back in among the trees like kids playing statues on the lawn. The day had turned as bleak as her search. Zoe forged on.

Up ahead, she heard hurried whispers and slowed her pace. Just beyond a large boulder, she saw four kids. One of them, a girl, was lying flat on the damp trail, her ear to the ground. Two of the boys were elbowing each other, sloshing their canteens, and laughing. The other was tugging on the arm of the girl, who was resisting.

"Can you hear it, Gail?"

"Shhh!" she hissed angrily. "Stop it, Chip! Hey! I think I heard something!"

"What's going on?" Zoe stepped forward, and the smell of alcohol enveloped her like the fog.

The two ringleaders tried to make sober faces, but they were unable to carry it off. The other boy kept pulling at the girl on the ground, who blinked slowly upon seeing a sudden addition to their party. She ran her tongue around her cottony mouth and enunciated, "I'm listening to the Underground Railroad."

"Where did you kids get that liquor?"

One of the boys swaggered toward Zoe. His nose was flat, his cheeks round, his eyes light blue and almost lost under the over-hang of his brows. "We don't have to tell you nothing!"

"I'm afraid you do," Zoe said and flipped out her ID. "Do you know what a federal agent is?" she asked, in the best imitation of Agents Scully and Mulder that she could muster, figuring these kids would recognize the routine. She quickly flipped shut the ID before they thought to question why there was no badge, and before Zoe could think about penalties for such a ruse. Although, she told herself, she hadn't exactly claimed to be a fed. "You can tell me here, or you can tell me back in Russell Creek. It's your call."

"They stole it!" the boy positioned by Gail said, half ducking from an expected blow, but looking Zoe in the eye the whole time.

"Oh, geez, Chip! Nice going!" spat the boy with the swagger.

"I'm only going to ask you one more time. Where did you get it?"

The smaller of the ringleaders licked his lips. "My brother won't even miss it. He won't mind that we took it."

Zoe held out her hand. "Give me that canteen." She did not

need to take a whiff that close to the stuff. Already, she felt as if she had breathed acid fumes. "This is white mule, isn't it?"

The boy with the flat nose squinted, making his eyes completely disappear. "How'm I supposed to know?"

"Tell her, D.B," urged Chip. "She's going to arrest us!"

"Shut up, Chip," D.B. warned. "She's just one person. There are four of us."

He smiled and raised his fists, feigned a swing at her, laughed. Muscles reacting without having to think about the movements required, long training paying off, Zoe had the boy on his back before the others could react. The evidence leaked out of the canteen where Zoe had dropped it a foot or two away.

"Now, where did this stuff come from? Don't you know there are reports that three people have already gone blind from drinking it?"

That remark finished wiping the smirk off D.B.'s face. But it was his friend who said, "He got it from Billy, over at the Ordinary."

"Shut up!" D.B. screamed. He seemed on the verge of losing control, so Zoe put her forearm under his chin, pinning him down.

"Do you know what the penalty is for assaulting a federal officer?"

"I'm a kid," he said. The bravado was gone.

"It doesn't matter. You'd be tried as an adult." Zoe thought that by this time her nose should have been long enough to prop her up. She skewered the other boy with her glance. "Billy at the Ordinary?"

"Yeah. Billy Cook the cook," he said, unable to hide a smile.

Gingerly, she eased herself away from D.B. and stood up, simultaneously producing her notebook and pen. "I'll need your names and addresses. Your brother's, too."

Chip tentatively asked, "Are you going to arrest us?"

"Not as long as you cooperate."

Ear still pressed to the packed dirt of the path, oblivious of the action that had occurred around her, Gail suddenly screamed, "Shh! Here it comes!"

By the time Zoe reached the phone outside the Ordinary, her knees quivered like aspen trees. She didn't believe in running for exercise, and now she was paying the price for that particular tenet of her lifestyle. It felt as if she were standing in a bowl of jelly during an earthquake.

She left a message for Ethan and then walked, rather stiff-legged, into the Ordinary, feeling like the sheriff in *High Noon*.

Ruth began to smile when she saw Zoe, but the expression bled away like hot wax off a candle. "What is it? Are you all right?"

"I need to talk to your nephew Billy, Ruth." Until Zoe heard his last name, she hadn't realized he was family to Ruth and Ardell.

The older woman gestured toward the dark, roped-off back corner of the Ordinary. "The diner is closed right now. The church holds a dinner, and we don't compete with that. Ardell's down there helping out, getting ready. What do you need Billy for?"

"Where is he?"

"He has a little apartment just under ours. It's out back. I'll show you."

"Just tell me where it is. I'll find it."

"Has something happened?"

There were no further questions as Ruth took Zoe straight to Billy's door. The apartment was, indeed, a small space, seemingly tucked under the balcony upstairs. Ruth rapped with the flat of her hand. "Billy?"

Wearing a rumpled T-shirt and jeans, Billy answered the door yawning and rubbing at his eyes. "I told you I didn't get much sleep last night, Aunt Ruth. And I've got a date tonight."

Zoe walked by him and entered the place. It looked like a motel room from the 1950s. A double bed, its covers thrown back, took up most of the space. There were two sailing prints on the reed papered walls. The television rested on an end table, and the lone lamp glowed bleakly on a table between the far wall and the bed. Straight through, the bathroom door stood open. Zoe took a step in there, just to be sure no one lurked around the corner.

"Billy," Zoe said, "all I want to know is if you sold white mule to Patrick Rourke just before he died. I'm not accusing you of anything else. Was the moonshine that was found in Rourke's truck supplied by you?"

His eyes slid to his great-aunt and then back to Zoe.

"Billy, you're not!" Ruth said, her hand to her mouth.

"I just had a couple of gallons," he said in pleading tones. "You know I won't touch the stuff, Aunt Ruth. But I did a friend a favor, and he gave me a few jars. I couldn't just throw it out, so I sold it to some guys I know. Patrick saw me do it. So I gave him his. I didn't charge him or nothin'. That's all there was to it. I did it then, but I wouldn't do it again. I swear, Aunt Ruth. I swear!"

Ruth sank down on the bed. "Billy, what are your parents going to say?"

"When did you give it to him?" Zoe asked.

He scratched his stomach. "On a Tuesday, I think? It was the night before he disappeared, whenever that was. That was the last time he got it. He got it a couple of times before that, too."

"How much did you give him?"

"Two whole quart jars. Well, a little bit at a time. I'd pour it into his travel mug instead of coffee. Then he'd kind of wink at me and leave. Like it was our secret."

"Did he come in regularly for it?"

"To get the mule? I guess. I didn't really keep track."

"And how much did you give him altogether?"

"I told you. A whole half gallon! Two quart jars."

"What happened to the empty jars?"

He shrugged. "I probably washed them and put them in the pantry upstairs. I think Aunt Ruth already used them for canning her apples. Why?"

"Why didn't he just take the jars with him?"

"Duh! Because he didn't want to be caught driving with an open container. He thought the police had it in for him. They'd gotten him for speeding a couple of times, he said. If they saw booze in the cab, too, he'd have had the book thrown at him. No way he wanted that. That was why he asked me to put it in the travel mug."

"Who's the friend you got the moonshine from?"

Billy raised his hands and backed away from Zoe. "No way. I can't tell you that."

"What would happen if you did?"

He smiled and shook his head. "My daddy always told me not to rat on a friend."

"It's no friend who sets you up like that."

Ethan showed up at Zoe's house after dark, bringing with him a whiff of wind and rain. He sank into the sofa with a sigh. While he ate without tasting a dinner Zoe had composed from bits of leftovers, he told her about the state police search of the Ordinary that had been conducted that evening.

"They looked everywhere, including all the guest rooms, which probably won't be great for repeat business. They even went down into that cellar. And examined all the outbuildings. There was nothing. Not even the empty jars. Billy was very cooperative, but Ruth and Ardell kept telling everyone they were wasting their time. If Billy is selling the stuff, I don't have the slightest idea where he keeps it."

"Was his home checked, too?"

"Oh, yeah. His father works for the Treasury Department, in D.C., comes home on weekends. He was none too happy to hear that someone thought there might be a still on his property."

Zoe enjoyed the irony even as she empathized with the situation. "What a headline that would make!"

He shrugged. "I was too tired to worry about it. This is good. What's this meatlike stuff that's not soy?"

"Seitan. Wheat meat. Ethan, has that guy who broke up the Ordinary been caught yet? What was his name? The one who was looking for his wife. He claimed she'd run away."

"Otis. Craig Otis. I haven't heard another peep out of him. There's a stop out on him, but who knows where he's gone to."

Ethan swiped at his mouth with his napkin. "What made you think of him?"

"You have to admit it's funny that two women disappear around the same time, both also have husbands who disappear, for a while, anyway, and—"

Ethan shook his head, saying, "Two women leave their husbands. The husband of one turns up dead. The husband of the other turns up and vandalizes a store. Women do leave their husbands. These instances just happened in close succession. Coincidence."

"But—" This time it was the phone that interrupted her. She sat still, waiting for the machine to take it.

Getting up, Ethan said, "It might be for me. The damn cellular doesn't seem to be working. Hello? . . . Hold on."

She took the proffered phone. "Hello? This is Zoe Kergulin." She was reaching in her back pocket for the notebook and pen that she usually carried, but she discovered she must have left them in the other room on her desk. Anticipating her need, Ethan wordlessly handed her his.

"Excuse me, ma'am, but are you the private detective who's been looking for Robert Rowder?"

Zoe's excitement caught Ethan's eye. "Yes. Are you Robert Rowder?"

The man laughed. "No, ma'am. But I'm his son, Ted. You left a message on my daughter's answering machine a day or two ago. She lives in La Jolla, over in California. She gave me a call here in Santa Fe and told me your message. I told her I'd look into it, and that's what I'm doing. What business do you have with my dad?"

After the explanation about the rings, glossing over the exact circumstance of finding the one she had found, Zoe said, "Mr. Rowder, is your father still alive?"

"He sure is. He lives in a nursing home not five minutes away from my house. I see him just about every day. Me and my wife both. He don't always know us, though."

"Do you know if he might have a garnet ring?"

"Sure he does. He's had it his whole life. It's a little big for him now, but he still won't take it off. They've had some thefts over at the home. Nothing big, but my wife was kind of worried about him losing that thing, so she bought him a ring guard. You know, it kind of makes the ring smaller? He wouldn't even take it off to let her put that on."

"Do you know the circumstances of how he got the ring?"

"It's his class ring. From high school graduation . . . Well, that's the story he used to tell us when we were kids. Now he says he won it in a poker game."

"Your father did used to work for the railroad in West Virginia and was something of a preacher?"

"That's my dad. He still thinks he's a lay preacher, giving sermons up and down the halls."

"Does he ever say who he won the ring from?"

"Oh, that's just nonsense talking. None of it means anything."

"It might be important, though, Mr. Rowder. Did he ever mention any other members of that poker game?"

"Nope. He'll say, 'Beat three tens, sir, beat three tens.' But he won't tell me who he played with."

"Thank you very much. Your information has helped a lot."

"Uh, you're not asking me for money or anything, are you? Because if this is a scam, I should tell you that I have no intention of paying you one dime."

"It's no scam, Mr. Rowder. I'm only trying to find the owner of the ring. Now I know it's not your father. That's all I needed to know."

"It seems a heck of a lot of trouble to go to just to find someone who has a red ring. But good luck to you."

Zoe hung up the phone. Tearing off the sheet of paper she'd been writing on, she handed the notebook back to Ethan. "The ring isn't Robert Rowder's. That means that unless Nolan Woods gave his ring to someone else before he died, or unless someone else dug him up and left him in the woods, the ring I found belonged to Jack Lamb."

Ethan gently picked up Cherry Pie, the outgoing brown tabby, from his lap and set him on the sofa cushion as he rose. Carrying his dinner paraphernalia into the kitchen, Ethan said over his shoulder, "But Jack Lamb wasn't in Sinksville. He was in Charleston."

"Huntington. According to Alma Eskew, though, he came back at least once. Maybe he came back more than once. And maybe one of those times, he ended up dead and was left in the woods. Maybe it all has to do with that moonshine."

"Maybe he was simply buried there by his relatives in an old family plot. There would have been no reason to tell his ex-wife about it, seeing as how they separated under less than ideal circumstances, from what you've said."

"I'll have to see if the state issued a death certificate. Any idea yet how old those bones are?" Zoe stood in the kitchen doorway, having tired of shouting between rooms.

"I haven't heard a thing." He slipped his silverware into the dish drainer and turned toward the refrigerator, drying his hands on his pants. "Is there any of that chocolate cake left?"

Later, over a glass of homemade wine, Zoe couldn't stop thinking about the revelations of the day. Ethan had fallen asleep on the couch, and Zoe's soft mutterings and exclamations as she went over her notes were enough to bring his gentle snoring and sputtering to a stop. He struggled to a sitting position and shoved the cushion behind him.

"What?" he demanded grumpily.

She glanced at him, his tousled hair, the traces of shadow on his cheek. How could anyone, female or male, not find him appealing? She stifled an indulgent smile. He wouldn't appreciate it. "Maybe Craig Otis thinks that his wife and Patrick Rourke were having an affair. Maybe he killed Patrick Rourke to get even."

"And how did he conveniently dispose of the two women?"

"Maybe they saw the whole thing. Maybe they're hiding from him, scared of what they know he can do."

"So far, all we know is that he can make a store smell like a cider press."

His eyelids, which had been drifting slowly downward, like a helium balloon losing viability, suddenly shot open. "I wonder if anyone's checked his basement for a still. He's supposed to be a teetotaler, but couldn't that just be a ruse?"

"If that ring really does belong to Jack Lamb," Zoe mused,

finishing up her wine, "then we should try to find the cemetery so he can be reburied. The rest of those bones could have washed away years ago. Floods, mine drainage. What a mess."

Ethan yawned, making Zoe yawn, too. "I'll get in touch with the state police. They may not want to pursue it if it's not a murder investigation."

"You want to spend the night?" Zoe asked, although Ethan was already beginning to snore again. "I haven't changed the sheets in the guest room, but you were the last to use the bed, so . . . Ethan?"

Before she turned out the light, she threw an afghan over him and Cherry Pie, sleeping nose to tail in his lap again, and kissed him gently on his whisker-rough cheek.

Zoe slipped a folded envelope from her jeans pocket and slid it under Ethan's blotter. She patted it a couple of times, as if to smooth it.

He had paused at his keyboard and watched silently as she'd entered his office and come to stand at his desk. "That isn't your last will and testament, is it?"

"I hope not. I want to go explore around the Ordinary in Sinksville tonight." She looked over her shoulder, making certain they were alone. "I thought a door or two that would usually be locked might just be unlocked tonight. Nothing you really need to know about, and neither do the people who review my p.i. license. Unless you don't hear from me by ten tomorrow morning. In that case, I would greatly appreciate it if you'd read what's in there. Otherwise, I'll just collect it in the morning and be on my way."

"What if you get killed?"

"I'll ask someone else, if you want."

"No." He fingered the edge of the envelope that stuck out from the blotter. "I could go with you."

"If you come, who's going to be around to arrest me? I'll be okay, Ethan."

"This reminds me of those secret agent games we used to play when we were kids. Those always gave me the willies, too." With effort, he tore his fingers from the envelope. "Ten tomorrow morning, then. But please make damn sure I hear from you."

In spite of the darkness, it was the quickest trip to Sinksville Zoe had made. She had arranged to leave her car at Alma Eskew's house. Alma was away at work at the video store when Zoe pulled up, and Zoe figured Alma would probably be sleeping by the time she left.

Zoe followed the road into town, sneaking into the trees when she heard a car. At eleven-thirty, there wasn't much traffic, and what few cars there were presented her ample opportunity to hide before they could spot her in their headlights. She could have taken the Pioneer Trail and come upon the Ordinary from the back, but it was the longer route, and the footing was too uneven in the dark. Her legs were feeling much recovered from her trek the day before, but she still opted for the road. It was more open, and gave her greater opportunities to see what might be coming up from behind.

In a little over half an hour, she stood plastered to the wall at the side of the Ordinary. There were no lights from the rooms above and only the blue glow of a television from Billy Cook's room around back. She didn't know if he was awake or not, but at least she knew where he was.

Zoe opened her day pack and removed the knee pads she'd brought along. She slipped them on and found the thin flashlight, its beam naturally narrow and bright. After making sure there was no one in the bathrooms behind her or about on the street, she slipped over to the door, carefully settling the pack beside her.

Using the flashlight, she examined the lock. She had noticed the dead bolt earlier and had come prepared to deal with it if she had to. She had been hoping it was there mainly for decoration, but not in use. So often since she had moved back to West Virginia, she had seen people install locks without using them, and she had been counting on Ruth and Ardell to do the same. Unfortunately, the dead bolt was securely in place. Zoe set to work on it, using the implements from her pack.

When she left the employ of the Justice Department, she took nothing with her except what she had learned during more than ten years of service. All her current tools had been self-acquired or self-developed, and adjusted over time. Her experience served her well, though, and within a few minutes, she was stowing her equipment and slipping inside the Ordinary.

During previous visits, she hadn't seen any motion detectors or alarm equipment, but just to be sure, she crouched by the front door, waiting, for several minutes more. Nothing stirred upstairs. No telephone rang to alert the tenants that a silent alarm had been tripped. If it was ringing in the police station, she would still have plenty of time to see what she wanted to see before anyone got there. Ethan's county police had only a skeleton crew out at that time of the night.

Still, she waited. Even straining, she couldn't hear the drone of the television from Billy's room. Either the old walls were very thick, or he had turned it off. She was hoping for the former.

Zoe had come because the Ordinary was the focus of too much that was going on for it to be attributed merely to coincidence. Susan Rourke had spent some time there, especially as a child. The search for her had been centered there, despite the fact that she had not lived there for some while. Her estranged husband, Patrick, had shown up there the night before he had disappeared. Craig Otis, husband of the second woman who was missing, had also made his way to the Ordinary, on the strength of no more than an errant brochure.

So, as Zoe's eyes adjusted to the darkness, she surveyed the deep shadows and wild shapes. Then she set off across the floor. Her immediate destination was the area where Craig Otis had done his vandalism with the apple cider vinegar.

As she had helped Ardell and Ruth clean up the floor, she had noticed a series of repeated scratches. At the time, she hadn't given them much thought. Now, though, it seemed to Zoe that they might be significant.

The glass case that Franklin Taylor had carried over the mountains had once stood in this store. Either Ardell or Ruth had told her that it had to be moved in order to get to the cellar. If that were true, why were the scratches toward the front of the store instead of the rear, where the cellar was? That glass case had no casters, so it had to have made marks when it was moved.

If it had rested on a rug, and the entire rug had to be tugged in order to budge the display case, then what had caused the gouges up front in the floor?

It wasn't a puzzle that the weight of the world rested on, but it was big enough to snag at the material of Zoe's thinking processes. And maybe, just maybe, by pulling at the loose thread it produced, something important would unravel.

Adjusting the knee pads, Zoe crawled toward the area, which still smelled vaguely of rotted apples. Wending her way around oversized baskets and bushels, making sure to pick up her feet as she crossed extension cords, and taking care not to bump into the seemingly haphazard arrangement of toys and camping gear too big to fit in baskets, she finally reached the area where she had glimpsed the scratches on the floor.

After sweeping up the broken glass, Ruth had hurriedly replaced the damp rug. Perhaps that was what drew Zoe's attention to the gouges now.

The shuffling of slippered feet overhead made Zoe freeze in position, straining her ears toward the slightest sound that would mean she was going to have company in the store. Despite all the time she had spent in this place, she was surprised to realize she had no idea where the staircase was that linked Ruth and Ardell's apartment with the lower level. For all she knew, it could be behind a door just a few feet away.

Eventually, a toilet flushed, water ran, and the slippers slapped the bare hardwood floor. Zoe didn't quite hear bedsprings sigh, but the footsteps stopped. In a few minutes, the stillness cushioned the darkness once again.

Zoe reached the edge of the rug. Crawling to its far side, she moved several small display tables and the baskets they contained. Cautiously shifting the loads, she mentally fixed the spots where they had been so she could replace each one precisely when she finished her search.

At last there was enough room to fold back the rug and reveal the scarred floor. Using the narrow beam of light and her fingers, she explored the deep scratches.

Two sets of them, about a foot apart, arced across the floor, as if only one end of the case had been swiveled out and then back again.

From her knees, she slid an antique wicker rocking chair out of the way and heard the soft crunch as it hit a bushel. Again, she paused and waited to hear if anyone else was listening.

Coldness touched the bare skin of her back, where she assumed her sweater had ridden up, but when she reached around to pull it down, she found the skin was securely covered. She shivered, laughed silently at unreasonable fears, and got back to uncovering the floor.

She hoped to find a round, flat handle, similar to the one on the trapdoor in the back of the store. The almost hollow sound she had heard when she knocked on the wall where the wreath had rested had come back to tap at her mind, and Zoe had managed to convince herself that a second hidden cellar must exist. She had outlined a vague hope that perhaps she would find Susan Rourke huddled down there among dust and cobwebs.

She folded back far more of the rug than should have been necessary, given the location of the scratches. There was no handle. Allowing her hip to sink to the floor, she sat and thought. If there wasn't a second trapdoor, then why the scratches on the floor?

Zoe crawled back over the area she had revealed, using the flashlight and then her hand to painstakingly search the floor inch by inch for any anomalies. Again she found nothing.

Stopping once more to ponder before admitting defeat, she let her finger fall into a knothole in the floor. It came to rest against something cold and metallic: a bar, or perhaps a latch. The hole wasn't big enough to let her get a finger around the bar to tug at it, so she pushed it to one side and heard a corresponding click in the floor.

The flashlight revealed a section of the floor that was raised just enough to fit fingers under. The door was counterbalanced and well-maintained, opening easily without a sound. Beneath her feet, the flashlight revealed stairs similar to the set in the other cellar. The beam was too narrow to show what might lie beyond the stairs, so she grabbed her backpack, inadvertently hit the rocking chair with her thigh, and prepared to descend into the darkness.

No creak accompanied a foot on the stairs, even when Zoe transferred her full weight to the downside leg. No dust crept into unsuspecting nasal cavities. No grit layered the thin handrail. This place was as pristine as its complement was decrepit.

The floor was carpeted in a thick pile, no doubt to absorb noise as well as keep out the cold.

A twin bed was fully made up in one corner. Checking under the spread, Zoe saw a feather pillow, blanket, and sheets. Two more blankets lay folded at the foot of the bed. A lacy dust ruffle stuck out below. Lifting it up, Zoe could see nothing underneath the bed—not even dust bunnies. Susan Rourke was definitely not hiding under there.

Beside the bed was a nightstand and a lamp. The drawers of the nightstand held a variety of candy bars, well-thumbed novels, and comic books. In the middle of the room sat an unplugged space heater, angled toward the twin bed. In the opposite corner were bunk beds, one on top of the other. They, too, were made, but they lacked the extra touches such as the feather pillow and bedspread. At their foot, a hole had been kicked into the drywall, exposing sagging pieces of that stuff and the silver foil of insulation. Above it was another hole, which was at a height to have been made by a fist. On the right side of that hole, a brown rusty stain had dried on a piece of jagged drywall.

At the foot of the twin bed was a closet, which turned out to be a small washroom, with toilet, shower, and basin. A door beside it revealed the actual closet, of the walk-in variety. The flashlight beam fell on dresses and pants hung tightly on a rod, with size markers separating them, as if they were displayed in a store. Shelves were piled with sweaters and shirts, and a few winter coats hung from hooks against the far wall. Boxes beneath them held scarves and gloves, a variety of comfortable shoes and boots, and wallets. The wallets were empty, and like the clothes, all appeared to be new.

The fourth wall of the main room held a large, framed print of flowers. Underneath it was a small end table on casters. Inside the end table, Zoe found individual boxes of cereal, boxes of long-shelf-life milk, juice boxes, crackers, and individual containers of peanut butter and jelly. Plastic utensils nestled in a box in the front corner.

Zoe checked behind the framed print. There was a hole back there, an opening like a knothole, just big enough for a finger to slip into and move the latch.

The wall swiveled about an inch or two on a central pivot. Once again, there was room to grab hold of the edge and swing it open. The little end table trundled out of the way with the motion of the wall. A blast of cold air entered the room.

A smaller passageway led from the room. Its floor was packed earth, and its walls were mostly rock and dirt and timbers that supported the weight of the roof. With some foreboding, Zoe stepped into the narrower, danker chamber. The flashlight beam showed only unlimited darkness ahead. Despite the sense of doom that seemed to emanate from the darkness, there was no way Zoe could leave it unexplored.

It was more than two hundred steps long. The entire way, the ceiling was high enough for her to walk upright. In places where the passage floor threatened to get muddy, boards had been laid. Although there was dirt, and tons of it, all around her, she did not feel claustrophobic. The passage was wide enough for two to walk beside each other. A cool breeze steadily wafted through, carrying a pine scent. Flower beds weren't dug as nicely as this passageway.

Underground Railroad, her mind whispered repeatedly. Underground Railroad. It was the stuff of legend.

At the end of the passageway was a ladder, a landing, and a shadowy, louvred door. A simple latch held the door closed. There was no visible lock. The door opened inward, and Zoe stepped out into the night, slipping her pack between the door and the jamb to ensure a way back in, just in case the door locked shut from the inside.

All around her, trees whispered as they swayed in the breeze. A tall hemlock shielded the door on one side, and a boulder sat strategically on the other. Running the flashlight beam over the surface of the rock, Zoe saw lichen, clinging like flaking greenish paint to its side. There was also a smear of brown that had dripped and dried. She followed the drip down the side of the boulder and found another smear just below it.

If someone had emerged from that door, or perhaps, gone in that way, there was a very small space in which to maneuver. With the boulder cutting off mobility on one side, the only way out was around the hemlock. If someone had been waiting for someone else to come out of the tunnel, it wouldn't be hard to determine just where they would step away from the shelter of the tree. Even in darkness, it would be difficult to miss, especially from close range.

Thinking of that, Zoe took a step back toward the door. What if there were someone watching that back door tonight?

She dropped to her knees and waited, surveying the forest from beneath that evergreen, watching to see what moved, listening to hear breathing besides her own. There was a small rustling in the leaves, which stopped abruptly. Then it began again, a few inches to the right of where it had been. A mouse, perhaps, its actions distorted out of proportion by the dead leaves and Zoe's imagination.

She crawled out from behind the tree, and after a few feet, stood up. Behind her and through the trees, she saw a meadow lit in the silvery radiance of moonlight filtered through clouds. At the edge of the field was a large dark outline that had to be the Ordinary. Beside it, several small cabins trailed like a line of ducklings. Those were the motel rooms. It looked as if the last cabin in the row was directly across from her current position. Beyond the cabins stood the mountain where she and Ruth had found the ring with the red stone, and somewhere beyond her sight stood Laurel Taylor's house.

Upon closer examination, the door did appear to have a simple lock that worked automatically when the door was shut. No casual passerby could enter, although anyone inside would not need a key to get out. She laughed to herself at the thought of a casual passerby out in the middle of nowhere. Chances were the door would not be found unless someone was looking for it.

Zoe stepped back inside, grabbing the pack and pushing the door shut behind her. Making her way back to the little room was easy enough. The passageway seemed shorter now that she knew where it ended.

Just before the spot where the wall angled out into the passageway, the place where she had stepped through from room to tunnel, she saw several wooden cases piled. They had been hidden behind the wall when it swung open, but now she could not miss seeing them.

Curious, she lifted the lid of the top one. Inside were quart mason jars, packed in straw and stacked double. Upon prying the lid off one of them, she caught the unmistakable whiff of liquor.

A quick survey showed that the other crates were similarly packed. Zoe was already well over the time she had calculated she could safely spend in the Ordinary without being detected, and she wasn't anxious to push her luck further.

On the other hand, she was so close to finding the source of the moonshine that she couldn't simply walk away.

To the right of the crates was another small recess. Stepping into it, Zoe could see from the pattern of dirt on the floor that a door must swing open from here. She searched with her weakening flashlight and with her fingertips, but she couldn't find the secret latch. She knew she was close to the still. It had to be in a room behind the door, carefully concealed and tended where no one else knew about it. No matter how she tried, however, the secret to opening the door stymied her. At last, she decided she had to leave it for the next foray.

Slipping back into the small furnished chamber, she pulled at the edge of the wall and was careful to get her fingers out of the way as it slid noiselessly into place. Even the latch was silent.

Zoe bounded softly up the stairs and stopped at the trapdoor to make sure the Ordinary was just as she had left it, when she heard a key in the dead bolt. Whoever it was would be bound to figure out that the lock was now open.

A tall figure stepped into the Ordinary and stayed by the door, blocking Zoe's hastily devised plan to dash out that way and escape.

"Ardell?" Ruth called out. Fear colored her tone. "Ardell? Is everything all right? What in heaven's name are you doing?"

As Ruth reached for a light switch, Zoe dove back down the

steps, pulling the trapdoor shut behind her. If Ruth hadn't spotted her yet, she might not know who the intruder was, but she sure as heck would know where she was.

Zoe fumbled at the latch behind the framed print, but the wall swung open easily enough. Dashing through, she found a rope pull on the other side and made sure the wall was secured behind her, although not before hearing Ruth shout, "Ardell! Who's down there? You answer me!"

Zoe ran with her left hand outstretched, flicking on the flashlight to get the general direction of the tunnel immediately in front of her and then flicking it off again to save what little reserve was left in the batteries.

Although on her last trip through she had marveled at the smoothness of the flooring, this time her feet found every imperfection. Her toe caught at the edge of a board, and her knee slammed down. Luckily, she was still wearing the pads, and they absorbed some of the impact. The second time it happened, though, she sprawled, scraping her face against the wall.

Only slightly shaken, Zoe found her feet. But she had lost the flashlight. She briefly felt around in the mud and dirt for it, but that only wasted time. So she once again stuck out her left hand, felt for the wall, and let it guide her toward the ladder.

Knowing there were no obstacles directly in front of her didn't mean the skeptical part of her mind would quite trust that assumption. It insisted on slowing her gait.

After traversing what seemed like twice as long a tunnel as she had been down before, she ran into the ladder with her elbow and clambered up. At the top, she waited briefly. She could see the louvred door in front of her but couldn't see what might be waiting outside. Her mind was flashing images of smeared blood, crimson fresh, on boulders.

Ducking to a crouch, she opened the door only as wide as she had to in order to get out. Her hand stayed on the door as a buffer to make sure it closed slowly and the lock clicked silently behind her.

She studied the area immediately around her. Although the landscape remained mostly monochromatic gray, she could easily make out the shapes of trees and rocks. The boulder appeared to be wedged tightly against the frame of the door on the ground, but it looked as if there might be space for her to squeeze through a few feet up. That way, she wouldn't have to come around the hemlock and announce her presence to the world, assuming the world was waiting for her over there.

Cautiously, she edged toward the boulder, keeping low. She and the pack wouldn't fit through the opening at the same time, so she shrugged out of it and rose, her back to the louvred door. On tiptoes, she placed the pack in the "V" of the opening and used her fingertips to push it through. It plopped softly when it hit the ground on the other side.

Zoe stretched a leg as far up the boulder as possible, using the doorframe against her back for leverage. When she reached a point where she could almost slip through, she felt a change in the air.

Taking a quick glance toward the hemlock, she discerned no shape even vaguely human. Even so, she leaped through the crack as if pursued. She landed hard, wrenching her knee. Spooked, she snatched up her little pack and took off.

At the edge of the trees, she turned, nervously scanning the woods behind her and the meadow in front. Despite the uncomfortable itch between her shoulder blades, Zoe saw nothing.

Gauging the distance to the cabins across the meadow, she dashed toward them, after a final glance back. Running in a form that would win her no medals, trying not to favor the aching leg she'd landed on, she concentrated on gaining, as quickly as possible, the shelter the shadows of cabins offered.

"Just hold it!" a low voice growled, simultaneous with a grab of her arm so fierce it nearly jerked Zoe off her feet.

The moon was behind the man, making his features indistinguishable, but there was no mistaking his tone. "How the hell did you get out of there?" he demanded, grabbing hold of Zoe's other arm and shaking. "Where's the damn hidey-hole?"

Zoe groaned and doubled over. As she'd hoped, the man loosened his grip and took a startled step away from her. She wrenched herself free from his grasp by straightening quickly, sending the back of her head into the man's jaw. Although she saw stars as a result of the collision, it was enough to temporarily disable her attacker. With a surge that she imagined left a cloud of dust in her wake, Zoe sprinted past the cabins and toward the road.

Glancing up the street, in the direction of her distant car, Zoe saw lights ablaze outside the Ordinary. She couldn't go back that way. Not now. Not yet. Resignedly, she squared her shoulders and jogged off into Taylor's woods.

Zoe planned to stay in the cover of the trees, parallel the road, and make her way back past the Ordinary and on to Alma Eskew's house, where the Chevy was parked. But a large stream diverted her. It flowed perpendicular to the road before disappearing beneath it, forcing her to go deeper into the woods until she could find a place sufficiently safe to cross.

The air was cool, with a taste of coming frost. The cold seemed intensified because she was so weary. At last, she managed to find a spot shallow enough to cross and level enough so that she didn't risk breaking her neck to get down to it. The icy water flowed over her shoes and numbed the lower part of her leg. She splashed water on her face and urged her tired body on.

She had taken so many twists and turnings following the stream that she no longer had a good idea where the road was. Deciding to backtrack for a ways, she followed the water from the opposite bank. Once the road was located, she could get to her car, find a phone, assure Ethan that all was well, and ask him to hold that envelope until she could reclaim it.

In it, she had laid out her suspicions about Ruth and Ardell, and the secret cellar at the Ordinary.

She thought she had paused only for an instant, to check her bearings and catch her breath. But before she could take another step, a cold metal gun barrel was thrust against her temple, and an unyielding hand she recognized again grabbed hold of her, this time from behind. Roughly, she was turned around.

The man she faced was not tall, but he looked powerfully built. His chest was broad, his arms so big in diameter they tested the strength of the fabric of his shirt. He wore a down vest, and a brown winter jacket was strapped to the framed backpack on the ground beside him.

The man was clean-shaven, with black hair that curled tightly against his head. A wide nose flared above a full mouth. His eyes were pale, and they studied Zoe like a hawk spying his dinner.

"Just stand nice and still now. Any sudden movements and, who knows?" He didn't move the position of the gun but, left-handed, patted her down. He didn't have the expert touch of a cop, but he made sure she carried no hidden weapons.

"Look," Zoe pointed out, using her professional voice to drown out the panicked beating of her heart, "you're getting yourself in deeper trouble here. Let me go. I won't press charges."

The man grunted in reply. He moved the gun then, although Zoe still felt it pressing against her, like a shadow with substance.

"We're going that way," he said, gesturing briefly away from the road with the revolver. "Don't try any tricks. If you do, you die, and so does your friend."

My friend? Zoe thought. At first, she believed he was threatening her with harm to Ethan, but she soon figured there was no reason for the man to be talking about Ethan. Perhaps he had taken Susan Rourke hostage and still had her secreted in some old cabin. The picture that presented in her mind, although it was just as irrational as the previous thought, made her shiver and grit her teeth.

"Where are we going?" Zoe asked, shifting her weight from leg to leg, waiting for an opportunity.

After ordering her to take off the day pack, the man snatched it and tossed it into the underbrush, all the while keeping the revolver trained on Zoe.

"Look," Zoe said in a tired voice, "I don't know who you think I am, but you've made a mistake." Zoe tried again. "Before the last few days, I was never even in this part of the county."

"I don't know who you think you are, but I'm here to tell you that I want my wife back. And if I have to trade you and your friend for her, I will. If I have to kill you, I'll do that, too."

"You're Craig Otis."

"As if you didn't know. Start walking. That way." He nodded in the direction he meant, the revolver steady.

"Mr. Otis, I read in the paper that your wife had disappeared. That's the extent of my knowledge of her."

"Just keep walking. Turn to the left there, along that deer trail."

"What do you think happened to her, Mr. Otis?"

"I know you and your kind took her. And I know I want her back. And I know ain't no one else getting her if I can't have her." The flat of his hand pushed Zoe in the back, as if for emphasis, and she went down on one knee.

"Get up!" he screamed. "I'll shoot you right here! I swear it! I know what you're all saying I did. I hear the news. Who's going to listen to my side now? Huh? Who's going to believe me? I figure I can do anything, thanks to you. I have nothing else to lose!"

Zoe had heard almost the same words from Paul Martin when he'd called to demand to talk to Karen, and she had denied knowing where Karen was. This time looked as if it was going to end just as badly, and Zoe was fast running out of possible ways to stop it from happening all over again.

She stumbled back to her feet and kept moving. "Maybe I can help you find your wife, Mr. Otis. I'm a private investigator. I have contacts you wouldn't be able to reach."

His responding laugh was rancorous.

"You kidnapped her, you bitch! You think she would have done something like this on her own? She's due to have a baby! Why would she leave me now? Someone put some fool idea in her mind! She's weak that way. She needs someone to tell her what to do. But not a bitch like you! You're going to show me where she is. Or else!"

He shoved her again between the shoulder blades, but this time Zoe was ready. She dropped, braced herself with her hands, and kicked out with everything she had, catching Craig Otis in the stomach, trying to put enough force behind the blow for a direct hit to his solar plexus.

The revolver dropped as he did, and it went off as it bounced on the ground.

"Damn!" she heard Craig Otis swear, and without stopping to collect her breath, Zoe dove down the hillside. She wasn't sure where the bullet had gone. Maybe it had hit Craig Otis, maybe the ground. With the onslaught of adrenaline flooding through her, she couldn't even be sure that she hadn't been hit and wouldn't know until shock replaced the rush.

At the bottom of the slope, she struggled to her feet. Covered with shredded autumn leaves and mud, she splashed through a small stream and headed upslope on the other side. She had lost all sense of direction, but she still knew that behind her was where a bullet would come from.

At the top of the rolling hill, she paused for a moment. She thought someone was crashing through the brush behind her.

Plunging down the next hillside, she kept her feet under her most of the way.

This slope was longer than the previous one, and steeper. When her right foot snagged on a rock, she tumbled through leaves and mud down to the bottom of the slope. In a heap of arms and legs, she fought for the next breath, all the time anticipating a bullet.

It seemed more like long minutes than seconds before Zoe managed to struggle to her knees. The pads had torn off on her descent, her jeans had ripped, and she was sure that bare skin and blood mingled with the mud beneath her.

A twig snapped, but even that couldn't send enough impetus through her muscles to get her on her feet. With a strangled breath, she swung her eyes up, expecting to meet the barrel of a gun.

"Why do you suppose we keep running into each other?" a wry voice asked. It was Ruth, standing by the creek, her hands on her hips.

"Craig Otis is right behind me," Zoe gasped, trying to figure out how she could regain her feet. "He's got a gun. A revolver."

Ruth took her by the arm and tugged with both hands. "You look as right a mess as I feel," she grunted. "Can you keep to your feet? Better follow me. There's a cave not far from here. We can rest there safely until he leaves the area."

"Where did you come from?"

"He tied me to a tree after I followed you out the tunnel. Guess he reckoned an old woman wouldn't be much of a threat to him, and he didn't tie me very tightly. I thought he might go for Ardell next, and I wanted to make sure he didn't hurt her. I'd seen him light out toward town after tying me, and I was just trying to follow. I didn't figure you'd be the one I'd find. You okay?"

Zoe decided she was feeling pretty good, considering. "I'll

keep up. But I think we should head back to Sinksville. It's dangerous to stay out here."

"Zoe, I don't know if you heard me, but I've been in these woods most of the night, and I've been walking steady, even running part of the time. There's no way I'm going to make it back to Sinksville without a rest. I think we can count on him looking for us now, and not going to bother Ardell. Since that's the case, I think we'd better take shelter. We're both about ready to drop."

The drizzle began before they reached Ruth's cave. By the time they clawed their way up the embankment and shoved behind the overgrown rhododendron that camouflaged the entrance, a full-scale downpour was in progress. The rain would obliterate their trail, but it would also obscure any sound of pursuit, or of rescue.

Soaked through, Ruth and Zoe crouched shoulder to shoulder in the small space, trying to share body heat. The thought of hypothermia danced briefly through Zoe's mind, but she cast it out. She thought longingly of the space blanket in the pack Craig Otis had tossed away.

"You wouldn't happen to be carrying any matches, would you?" Ruth asked in a flat tone.

"I've got a pocket knife, my keys, ID, and a few dollars. I could try rubbing two pennies together." Zoe winced as she tried to get comfortable. Ruth's arm came around her shoulders and tucked her in close.

"Oh, well. I guess our bodies will heat up this space eventually." Zoe nodded.

Ruth continued, "You've got things figured out, don't you?" Her hand squeezed Zoe's shoulder.

Zoe's teeth chattered, but she persevered. "I know it was Jack

Lamb's ring I found. He was wearing it when he was killed. You and Ardell killed him, didn't you? And you buried him somewhere around that place where you and I stopped that day."

Ruth rearranged herself so both hands grasped Zoe's shoulders. "You're thinking we just did away with him? Let me tell you about that time, Zoe. That man was stalking Ardell—even though we didn't have a name for it then—not even letting her draw breath without him there to tell her when and how much! She tried to tell him to go away, but he wouldn't listen, thought she didn't know her own mind. He was just about driving her crazy. I was so afraid she was going to do something awful."

"Kill him, you mean?"

"No, kill herself, I mean! She was at the end of her rope, and what could she do? We couldn't leave! We had our jobs at the Ordinary, and jobs weren't that easy to come by then.

"One night, I heard Ardell cry out. The sound woke me right up, even though it was gone by the time I opened my eyes. It was the kind of noise you make when you wake from a nightmare. I thought Ardell had had a bad dream, and I thought she probably could use some comforting. So I got out of bed without even putting on my robe or slippers, and I tapped on her door and opened it, and there was Jack Lamb on top of her, one hand to her throat, the other holding what was left of her nightgown.

"Well, what would you have done, Zoe, if it had been your sister?"

Ruth's hands fell to her lap in two clenched fists. "I grabbed the poker from the fireplace, and I hit him. And I didn't stop hitting him. And when my arm was too tired to lift the poker, he was dead.

"I drew a hot bath for Ardell, washed her up good, put her into a clean nightgown, and tucked her into my bed. I didn't want to leave her, Zoe. It was the last thing in the world I wanted to do, but I had to take care of the body. You know what would have happened if we'd called the police and told the truth?"

Zoe nodded, colder, if possible, than she'd been before.

"I'd have ended up in jail, which maybe I could have taken. But who would have looked after my sister? There were no rape crisis centers then, no laws that said a man couldn't rape his own wife. I didn't think twice about it. I just concentrated on hiding what had happened. That car of his seemed like it would be a fitting tomb for him. He was damn proud of that thing. It was so fancy. I thought it would hold him forever."

"How did you manage to get it so far into the woods?" Zoe asked, trying to ignore a pain digging its way deep into her side.

"Oh, Franklin had cut a logging road up the mountain some. He didn't clear cut, just took enough trees for a couple of buildings. But I drove up there a ways. Then I got out and just let that car roll down the mountainside. Over the years, I pictured Jack Lamb still sitting in that car, staring at the vines and the brambles. But as soon as you found that ring of his, Zoe, I knew that damn car had rusted away around him, and my secret wasn't secret anymore." She paused and ruefully shook her head. "Cars back then rusted a whole lot quicker than they do now, that's for sure."

"What happened to Ardell, is that what gave you the idea about the Underground Railroad?"

Ruth smiled, although her lips were tinged with blue. "You figured that out, did you?"

"You help women escape from abusive partners. You helped—"

Zoe groped for Craig Otis's wife's name, and Ruth quickly supplied, "Ora Lee Otis."

"And you must have helped Susan Rourke, too. That's why there's been no trace of her. Where do they go from here?"

Ruth's smile got wider. "All over, Zoe. All over. When Ardell and I started helping women along, we could only send them to people we knew personally. Now, there's a whole network of people. We even have contacts in women's shelters across the country. If we need to, we can house a woman from West Virginia in a shelter in Georgia or even Colorado. Her abuser will never find her. It's a beautiful system."

"Obviously, killing isn't part of the plan. But Patrick Rourke found the hidden room, didn't he? He's the one who punched the holes in the walls, isn't he? That's how he bloodied his knuckles. Did he find Susan? Is that why you killed him?"

A bolt of lightning crackled nearby, the thunder so close on its heels that Zoe had to lean close to hear Ruth's reply.

"I didn't kill Patrick Rourke, Zoe!"

"Ardell killed him?"

Ruth's eyes went to heaven, and her lips disappeared between her teeth. "We never killed him, Zoe! I knew that once you found the ring and figured out who it belonged to, they'd come arrest Ardell and me, thinking that if we were involved in one death, we must be involved in the other. But we weren't the ones who killed Patrick!"

Zoe blew on her stiff fingers and rubbed her hands together. "Who did kill him, then?"

"I wish I knew the answer to that one, Zoe. Ardell and I have thought long and hard on it, but we just don't know."

"But Patrick did find the secret room under the Ordinary, just the way I did. What happened after that?"

"Oh, he was a sly boots, that one. He hid himself behind the lunch counter one night after we closed the Ordinary, and he watched us go down there. Susan wasn't with us then, thank goodness. We hadn't brought her to the Ordinary. Patrick was there too often.

"But that night, he snuck down, and we caught him, by slamming the trapdoor shut. Then we had to think about what to do with him. How could we report him for breaking and entering a place that wasn't supposed to exist? It would mean the end of everything! Ardell thought maybe we could put some of her sleeping pills in some food, and once he'd eaten it, we could carry him out and drive him back home. We could go on vacation for a month or two, close our stop temporarily. Who would believe the fool mutterings of a drunk? Or maybe he wouldn't remember any of it as real. The important thing was to get Susan away safely."

Zoe's eyes narrowed as her lips curved into a smile of discovery. "But Patrick found the secret door to the passageway, didn't he? And the liquor hidden behind it."

Ruth studied Zoe's face for some sign of judgment. "We went into the moonshine business to pay for the Railroad. Once Franklin gave up the still, we took it over. The demand was still high, and the profit good. There was no way we could have financed all of what we do just through the sales at the Ordinary."

"But the Ordinary was the perfect cover, wasn't it? You could order all kinds of things, as if you were going to sell them, when all along, they went with the women you were helping, to enable them to start a new life."

Ruth nodded. "That's it exactly. They couldn't take anything with them when they disappeared. Everything had to be new, even their names and the names of their children, if they had any."

"So Patrick found the moonshine, the white mule," Zoe said, picking up the story as if she had been there. "But he never did know where Susan was when she left him, when she moved in near my house, did he? She'd never been there before, so there was no way he could have figured it out. She saw the rental notice and took a chance, hoping he wouldn't be able to trace her there."

When Zoe had discovered the trashed trailer, it had struck her that the handmade quilt was on the floor in one piece in the face of the violence of the rest of the attack evident in the place, but what she had seen only began to make sense when she saw the undamaged heirloom again at Laurel's house. The quilt had deliberately been spared. A man in the heat of passion would not have given a moment's thought to saving a treasured quilt.

Zoe wanted to pace as the pieces fell into place, but there was barely room in the cave to sit upright, let alone stand. "You staged Susan's abduction from the trailer, didn't you, Ruth? You used her blood, just enough to make the handprints on the window. Just enough to enable the police to identify her and, as a matter of course, assume that her estranged husband was to blame. Actually, I was the one who did that first. I jumped right to the conclusion I was meant to, didn't I? That sure explains why there wasn't more blood spattered around the trailer."

Ruth nodded gleefully. "I knew you were capable. Go on!"

"Patrick got drunk on the moonshine, and probably went tearing around the passageway. He would have had no flashlight or candle, so he likely took quite a few tumbles. By the time he found the ladder at the end of the tunnel, he'd have worked himself up into quite a rage."

"Rage doesn't come close," Ruth nodded. "Since we had to get Susan out quickly and not through our usual route, it occurred to us, seeing as Patrick had found the white mule and was already drunk, he'd be in perfect shape for the police to pick him up and hold him for a while to question him about Susan's supposed murder. That would give us time to decommission the door to the underground room and hide the still. Best of all, it would get Susan safely away without Patrick having a chance of finding out where she was."

Zoe lowered her voice, just in case Craig Otis lingered nearby. "You had Ora Lee Otis scheduled to come in, didn't you? What were you going to do about her?"

Ruth shrugged. "We were going to get her away from her husband, however we had to. But first we had to take care of Susan."

"Where was Patrick's truck while all the commotion was going on underground?"

"Why, in the parking lot at the Ordinary, of course. Everyone seems to have a pickup truck these days, so it fit right in."

"Why didn't you get the moonshine out of his truck? Why let it be found?"

Ruth shook her head, and water dripped from strands of hair that had escaped the loose pinning. She shivered. "No one had the slightest idea Billy had been slipping him the mule. That was quite a revelation."

"Laurel wasn't a part of this, was she? How much have you told her?"

"She knows that her sister is safe, that she's with friends. Susan's already called Laurel, via a couple of scrambled conference call connections, so don't even try to have any calls traced. She'll be writing through others, and so will Laurel."

"That was your idea, wasn't it, to have Laurel offer to hire me? She'd seemed fine with things up until then. I knew something had changed."

Ruth raised her eyebrows and gave a little shrug. "I didn't think it would work, but you were pressing too hard."

Ruth cocked her head. "It sounds as if the rain is letting up. Shall we see if it's safe to head back for Sinksville?"

Zoe crawled out first, staying near ground level, peeking through the decimated foliage to make sure the way was clear. It was a struggle to get to her feet again, but it felt wonderful once she could stretch, painful or not.

Cautiously, helping each other down the slope, Ruth and Zoe headed back to Sinksville. The light was so gray that there was no way to tell what time of day it was.

Zoe hurried Ruth along. Now that they were moving again, she had a renewed determination to call Ethan before ten. Certain suspicions about Ruth and Ardell, which she had detailed in her letter, were wrong. Others outlined information she no longer wanted Ethan to know.

"Does Susan know Patrick Rourke is dead?"

"Of course she does. She's not a prisoner, you know."

"The police are looking for her."

"So let them look. There is no way that woman is ready to come back here now. She needs time to recover. That husband of hers beat her down until she thought she was worth nothing. You don't get over something like that very quickly."

"What kind of help will she get?"

"Believe it or not, she's already working. In a women's shelter. Under a different name and Social Security number. Even I couldn't find her, if that's what you're thinking. But my point is that she'll recover fastest by helping others in a similar situation. She won't tolerate others being treated the way she was. Eventually she'll make the connection, realize her strengths. And, when she's stronger, I think she'll be able to come back here, if that's what she wants."

"Will she be Susan Rourke then?"

"She'll be whoever and whatever she wants to be. Don't you see, there are all kinds of possibilities opening for Susan now. It's her decision now. Scary as that is for some, it's as it should be. I have no more right to direct her life than Patrick did."

They both slid down a short slope, hanging onto tree limbs and trunks when their feet couldn't get purchase. Zoe banged her shoulders a few more times and tried to believe the pain didn't even register anymore. Fog began creeping back like a fawning dog. It hid the women, but it also gave shelter to anyone pursuing them. They seemed a long distance from Sinksville.

"What part does that reporter Willa Fiore have in this?" Zoe asked. "Is she your propagandist?"

Ruth chuckled softly. "She's amazing, isn't she? I love to hear her tell that research about the Underground Railroad. She really believes that stuff about there being no Railroad. She's proud of her research and just can't stop trying to educate people. Maybe she would have been happier if she'd gone into teaching . . .

"Oh, she's one of us, all right, Zoe, but she generally works out of Russell Creek. She's not usually involved in the actual escape, but she helps women who need help find us, and she helps coordinate our operation. We did ask her to keep an eye on you initially, and we had her research your background, so we were relatively confident that you wouldn't go blabbing what you knew."

"What about the part that Craig Otis played? Did he really attack your store?"

"Perhaps we embellished a bit. He did break a jar of cider vinegar, though! Maybe it was an accident as he swung around to leave, but it seemed like a fortuitous circumstance. Ardell and I made the most of it."

"You wanted him to be picked up by the police so he wouldn't find the secret room the way Patrick Rourke had."

"That, and his wife. We had to keep her for a few days until she could make connections out of here. He'd been hanging around so close that we were afraid to breathe. When I came in last night and saw the trapdoor raised, I was certain he was the one down there. I thought for sure we were going to have another Patrick Rourke on our hands."

"But now he's desperate," Zoe said. "He believes the police think he's a crazed husband on the loose, and maybe a murderer to boot. Maybe it doesn't even matter to him anymore."

"We did stir him up, but it was only to get his wife safely away. When they leave is the time they're most likely to be killed, you know. We were trying to get him arrested."

"I hope it happens before he does manage to kill someone." Zoe shook her head. "So, how did Patrick Rourke end up dead that night?"

"Damned if I know, Zoe. When Ardell hadn't heard anything from the basement for a while, she went down to check the tunnel, and Patrick was gone. He'd found the way out. By the time she got back upstairs and into the Ordinary, his truck was gone, too.

"We could hardly call the police and report him missing, could we? We figured he was out rampaging around the county, and as soon as someone discovered Susan's trailer, he'd be jailed for a while." She repeated, "We didn't kill him, Zoe. I swear it!"

"Sheriff," Zoe said as she entered Ethan's office, her hands at shoulder height as if pushing open the doors to a cowboy saloon, "just hand over the envelope and no one gets hurt."

"I hope you had as sleepless a night as I did. I had the damn thing in one hand, the letter opener in the other, when you called." Grudgingly, he gave her the still-sealed envelope. "I guess you might as well sit and let me know what you found out."

"Did you get Craig Otis? How badly did he shoot himself?"

"The bullet grazed his shin. Nothing too serious. He could have killed you, Zoe."

She nodded. "Did you manage to get those records I asked you about?"

Reaching for two pages that had just popped out of the printer, he handed them across the desk to her. "That's all the dog-related crimes reported this year for Bickle and Feller Counties. Patrick Rourke's name appears nowhere. What were you looking for?"

"I don't know," she replied, her eye still scanning, still hoping to find a name she recognized. "The dogs keep sticking in my mind. Patrick was supposed to have been breeding those hounds. But Laurel and Dorsey had only three dogs, and all of them were males. If those were Patrick's, then what happened to the female? There had to have been at least one. Even Patrick couldn't have been that inept. I was hoping maybe he'd filed charges, or someone had filed charges against him . . .

"And this secret of Dorsey's, whatever it is . . . I thought maybe it had something to do with stealing dogs." She shifted in her chair, trying not to let the sharp pain that suddenly jabbed her show as a wince on her face. "Maybe Dorsey's involved in some dog dealing scheme. I don't know, Ethan. I was hoping a name would jump out at me from these pages." She shook them in futility.

"Not too many of those crimes involve kidnapping dogs," Ethan observed. "Most of 'em are people mistreating their own. If a dog is missing, it's not reported as a crime. Even if a person suspects the dog has been stolen, unless there's a ransom note or a corpse, most likely it's just reported as a missing animal. And we don't keep statistics on anything like that. Besides, Patrick Rourke could have sold the female. Maybe he had her put to sleep. Who knows?"

Zoe brightened. "Or maybe Dorsey's culling dogs from around the area. He could be finding new homes for animals he thinks are mistreated. Maybe he stole the females first and neglected to tell me."

"Ethan," a young officer interjected, standing uneasily in the doorway to the sheriff's office. Upon getting her superior's attention, she reported, "State police say they're calling in a crew with shovels. One of the surveillance teams at the Rourke house smelled something rotting this morning. It's in the neighbor's field, right next to the Rourke property. They've requested your presence at the scene."

Ethan grabbed his hat as he rose from behind the desk. "That'll be Susan Rourke's body," he said with a grim nod to Zoe. "She didn't get away. She came back, just like always, and he managed to kill her. Then your two friends, Ruth and Ardell, took care of him."

"No, Ethan," Zoe said, struggling to get out of her own chair.

In the doorway, he turned. "You okay?"

Perturbed at the unwillingness of her body to do the mundane things she usually took for granted, she nodded anyway. "Fine. But Ethan—"

He pointed a finger at her. "I want to talk to you later. And listen, if the judge sets Craig Otis free before trial, let's get some protection for you, okay?" He turned and was gone.

Zoe sat there perhaps a minute longer, her eyes straying off to one side or the other, focusing on nothing in Ethan's office, a line of concentration between her eyes. At last, she jumped from the chair, holding her side in surprise when pain ripped through her like an electric shock.

"Ethan!" she called, running to the doorway. "It's not Susan! It's—" By the time she reached the hallway, it was empty.

At Sam Bennett's house, a woman picked up the receiver.

"Hello," Zoe said. "May I speak to Mr. Bennett, please."

There was silence, followed by a flat, nasal voice asking, "Are you her?"

"Her?" Zoe asked.

"Her. The one wrecking my marriage. That you?"

"It's not me. My name is Zoe Kergulin. I'm a private investigator. I wanted to talk to Mr. Bennett about hunting dogs."

"Sure you do. You know he's eating himself up over those damn prize dogs. You give 'em back, and you give me my husband back."

"Ms. Bennett, it's very important I find your husband. Is he at work?"

"Are you sure you're not the one breaking up my marriage? Don't you be calling here no more. If he's left you now, then good! You deserve it, you bitch!"

With a slam of the phone, the line disconnected, and Zoe was left to stare at the receiver in her hand.

"Laurel! Dorsey! Let me in!" Zoe pounded on the wide-beamed door while the wind wrapped itself around her words and threw them down the mountainside. She tried the handle on the door, but it was locked.

Both the truck and the Saturn were in the parking area. Laurel and Dorsey had to be somewhere in the many acres surrounding the family home. It was a search Zoe didn't relish undertaking.

Listening intently for barking dogs but hearing nothing, she set off up the hillside in the direction of the abandoned farm where the hunting dogs had been hidden.

As aware of her unarmed state as if she had come naked to this place, Zoe walked with caution and in cover whenever possible. Along the way she picked up a fallen limb she could use for walking or for defense.

Meanwhile, clouds churned the sky, solidifying into a mass of gray and black, and the wind increased with each gust, whipping up dust and grit.

Zoe narrowed her eyes, wrapped an arm around her middle as if to protect herself from further harm, and set her pace.

Almost within sight of the stone house, she heard whimpering and followed it to find one of Laurel's dogs, Goodness or Mercy, huddled in a depression at the base of a boulder. One leg dripped blood, but that did not prevent the dog from baring his teeth at Zoe.

"It's okay, hon," she said, hanging onto the stick but holding out the other hand, palm up.

From the far side of the boulder came the other dog, equally upset, but seeming to be in one piece.

"It's okay, guys," Zoe repeated. "Where's your mom, boys? Where's Laurel?" She began to back up, slowly feeling her way, unwilling now to turn her back on the dogs. The hackles were raised on the uninjured dog, who was matching her, one pace forward for each she took backward.

When a rifle shot let loose nearby, Zoe forgot all about the dogs and her abused ribs, and dropped to the ground with the force of habit and long training.

"Dorsey!" she heard Laurel cry out, just before another report punctuated the wind.

Scrambling to her feet, Zoe managed a running shamble, keeping the barn between her and the stone house for as long as she could, not looking back to see if the uninjured dog still stalked her. Without realizing it, she crossed the narrow part of the path where she had taken a tumble. All of her attention was focused on what was going on within the old stone dwelling.

The door stood open, but the inside of the house was dark and ominously silent. Slipping up against the cold stone wall, Zoe watched the open doorway, her mind involuntarily flashing back to the disarray she had found at Susan Rourke's trailer.

"Did you kill him?" Zoe heard Laurel ask in a strangled voice.

"Shut up! Just shut your mouth!"

There was a shuffling of feet. Something hard hit something soft. A stifled cry of "No!" propelled Zoe through the doorway.

Inside, the darkness temporarily blinded her, and she stayed low and against the wall, trying to use to her advantage what little light leaked in from outside.

The last time she had been up against a man determined to kill, Paul Martin had murdered her best friend. Like a tornado that levels a town, that act had taken Zoe's ambition, her carefully nurtured dreams, and the friend who was as much family to her as any of her brothers and sisters, and blown them all away, scattering the wreckage to the elements like so much flotsam.

There was nothing Zoe could do now about any of that, but she was certain she could not allow Sam Bennett to do to Laurel Taylor what Paul Martin had done to her. Of its own accord, her hand reached frantically around her waist for the semiautomatic that she no longer wore.

Forcing down the panic that was relentlessly building like wave after wave up a beach at high tide, Zoe focused on what she had to do. She had no weapon, no communication, and no backup. And maybe she was already too late. Terror burbled up her throat.

A few feet away, a figure emerged from the shadowy darkness. Zoe saw a body on the floor, smooth back toward her. She reached out a hand and felt fur and faint warmth but, from her position, was unable to determine if the dog still lived or if the heat was leaking from his body like air from a punctured tire.

Laurel's pale face was the next thing Zoe discerned in the darkness. At the same instant, Laurel caught sight of her. The huge eyes of the younger woman flashed toward where the access to the upstairs had been boarded over.

Zoe nodded, hoping she got the message correctly, trying to convey with that one gesture that a professional had arrived, that Laurel was no longer alone. She squinted, trying to find movement where Laurel had indicated.

In the dark, Zoe felt around for the stick she had been carrying, but it was gone, lost somewhere between outside and in. A quick search of her pockets revealed her Swiss army knife, and her hand closed around it like a drowning sailor in shark-infested waters reaching for a lifeline. It wasn't much, and never before had she considered it a weapon, but it was all she had.

A fist hit the boarded-up wall of the staircase. Zoe jumped in response and almost lost her grip on the knife. Sam Bennett was moving past the staircase. If he turned toward the door, Zoe knew he would spot her. As it was, her breath sounded raspy and very loud in the small room. She had to act quickly, or it would be the end of not only her, but of Laurel and Dorsey and the dogs, too.

By feel, she inventoried her compact piece of equipment. There were two blades, a corkscrew, a can opener, two screw-drivers, a bottle opener, and a small saw. A toothpick and a pair of tweezers rounded out her arsenal. None of them would do her much good against a rifle.

She unfolded the knife blade before remembering, with a wry grimace, what one of the government self-defense instructors had counseled about how to survive a knife fight: Don't get involved in one.

She carefully bent the hinge of the larger blade and tucked it back into its casing. For a moment, she studied the weighty instrument in her palm. Surely its many quality accoutrements could not all fail to be of some use to her now.

Then an idea came to her. At one end of the small tool kit, she folded down the metal ring the retailers identified as a lanyard, and keeping the closed knife tight in her fist, she crept along the wall, taking careful breaths around the stabbing pain that no longer seemed to subside.

She hoped that by now Ethan would have gotten the message she had left. By now, he would know that what the state police had smelled was rotting dog flesh, not a murdered Susan Rourke.

By now, the team should have turned up the dead dogs that had once belonged to Patrick Rourke. By now, with luck, the reinforcements should be on their way to Laurel's house.

Somehow, by accident or design, Dorsey had taken Sam Bennett's dogs.

"Where the hell's the other one?" Bennett demanded, turning the rifle toward Laurel.

"No!" Laurel screamed and ducked her head.

Zoe lunged across the floor and jammed the still-closed knife hard between Bennett's shoulders, careful to keep her fingers from touching him and spoiling the effect. He froze, muscles stiffened.

She whispered, "Have you ever seen the damage a good nine millimeter Sig Sauer can do at close range?" She jabbed him again, harder, when he made no move to give up his weapon.

"You decide, Mr. Bennett," Zoe said hoarsely through teeth gritted to keep them from chattering. Her raspy breath made it sound as if she was as much over the edge as Bennett. Maybe it would work to her advantage. She knew, though, that if he decided to go ahead and shoot Laurel, there was nothing she could do about it. After that, he would turn the rifle on her.

For a moment, no one moved. Then, his rage barely stifled, Bennett raised the rifle and surrendered it behind himself to Zoe. Her knees shook as she grabbed it and, after a few tries, slipped the knife back into her pocket.

"Don't move. Not a muscle," she told Bennett, training the rifle on him. "Laurel!" she called out. "You okay?"

"Yes," Laurel replied shakily and stood up. "He shot Dorsey! And Goodness! I don't know where they are."

"Goodness was doing okay. Mercy was looking out for him. Find some rope or chain. Let's take care of Mr. Bennett, and then we can take care of Dorsey."

"Keep pressure on those wounds," Zoe cautioned, surprised to find herself short of breath. She dismissed her condition as a result of tying up Sam Bennett and helping haul Dorsey's limp, but living, body from the cold basement of the stone house.

Dorsey now lay on two dog beds, with dog blankets piled

atop him. Laurel leaned over him, a dish towel folded beneath her bloodied hands. The bullet had blazed through Dorsey's abdomen, doing who knew what kind of damage. Laurel pressed hard with the heels of her hands, but Zoe could see there was too much blood. Deliberately, she focused elsewhere.

Bennett squirmed in cold and discomfort, the leather of the dog collars they had used to bind him biting into his wrists and ankles.

Outside, the wind gusted in a roar, sending chill fingers through the house.

"Why did you kill Patrick Rourke's dogs?" Zoe asked. "Is that how all this started?"

Sullenly, Bennett replied, "I don't have to tell you nothing."

"You're right," Zoe said. "Maybe it would be better if you didn't. You've already killed Patrick Rourke in cold blood, and Dorsey here isn't looking too good . . ."

"Dorsey," Laurel whispered, echoing Zoe.

Zoe steeled herself. It had been an emotionless thing to say in front of Laurel, but she had been focused on prodding Bennett.

"It wasn't cold blood!" Bennett spat. "He ruined my bitch! She was purebred, with papers going back close to fifty years! That dog won every damn treeing contest I ever entered her in! I had orders for her pups for the next two years!

"One night, we were drinking, and Patrick, he tells me he can get ahold of his daddy's champion coonhound, and he asks me, do I want to mate him with my bitch. Hell, yes, I say! His own damn dogs weren't worth the food it took to feed them, but a Rourke hound was something different. He says his daddy is letting him run The Duke in some lodge contest that weekend. And he says he can arrange to mate the two during that time.

"I was working, so I didn't see it, but the vet confirms the bitch is pregnant. And a couple of weeks after that, when we're out drinking again, Patrick lets slip that his old man got mad at him, and he never did get the dog that weekend. And I say, 'Well, Patrick, then who did you mate with my bitch?'"

Zoe sat on the hearth. The barrel of the rifle slipped toward the ground, but Sam Bennett didn't notice. The weapon was heavy to hold, and Zoe kept her grip on it but allowed it to come to rest against her knee.

Bennett didn't even stop for breath. "Patrick, he smiles kind of sly-like, and he says, 'My blue hound.' That mangy mutt was no more hound than I am! Patrick, he says, 'Remember, I get pick of the litter!'

"He mates my prize dog with his shit! I went home right there and killed her myself. What good was she anymore? He ruined her!

"After that, I go over and kill his damn dogs, one after the next, saving the damn blue hound for last."

Bennett was breathing hard, and his eyes glowed strangely in the dim light of the house.

Zoe glanced toward Laurel. The younger woman's position hadn't changed, but Zoe couldn't tell if Dorsey was still breathing. She blinked and forced her attention back to Bennett.

She said, "But Patrick Rourke knew it was you who'd killed his dogs, didn't he? And he took your dogs to get back at you. And then you went over there and killed him."

"I didn't! I went over there to get my dogs back! But they were gone! And he was gone. I thought he was using my dogs! I went looking for him. First, I thought he was checking his traps. I knew where they were because I'd helped him set them out, but he wasn't there. Just that damn cat hissing and spitting at me. On the way out of Sinksville, I stopped at the Ordinary, and damned if I didn't see his truck in the parking lot!"

Laurel had begun crying softly, but Sam Bennett neither heard nor saw.

"I eased open the door and took his shotgun. I just took it, the way he took my dogs. I didn't even think about using the damn thing!

"The store was closing, so I knew he wasn't in there, but I figured he was in one of the cabins, making it with some girl. He used to do that sometimes. So I snuck around to that field in back to look in a few windows and find out which cabin he was in. But some of the curtains were drawn, and I couldn't tell which one he was in. So I fell back, figuring that from a distance I could keep an eye on all of them. When he came out, I'd have the bastard.

"But all of a sudden, I hear a ruckus behind me, and I turn around, and he's coming at me! He was stinking drunk, and he was yelling I don't know what, and he was coming right at me!"

It took some effort to breathe and talk at the same time, but Zoe said, "So you brought up the shotgun in self-defense and pulled the trigger." She leaned back against the fireplace wall.

"You would've done the same thing," Bennett claimed. "Anyone would. He was out of his mind. No one came to see what happened, so I carried him out to his truck and drove him out into the woods. After that, I cleaned up the cab real good. Then I walked back, picked up my truck, and went on my way."

"But why," Zoe said and paused as her mind suddenly shut down. She tried again. "Why come out here gunning for Laurel and Dorsey?"

"My damn dogs is why! I knew they weren't anywhere on Rourke's property or the cops would have come to talk to me. Hell, the collars all have ID." He held out his bound feet to show Zoe the metal ID strip attached to the leather. It showed only an 800 number, a number to identify the dog, and a single word, "Reward."

"Besides," Bennett continued, "there's a microchip under the skin of each one. That's for identifying the dogs, too.

"When the cops didn't show, though, I thought you must have the dogs. When you asked Wyatt and me to meet you at that bar, you were reading that book about hounds. I figured you were letting me know, and you'd be after me for something.

"So I went to the vet's office to find out exactly what the microchips say and to find out how to scan them. I was going to turn the tables on you and have you arrested for stealing, and I wanted to make sure I could prove those dogs belonged to me. But while I was at the vet's, I heard some kids talking about fixing dogs, real proud-like, and I heard them say Patrick Rourke's name, and I knew then that they were the ones who had my dogs. It only took a little more work to find them."

"Why not go to the police?" Zoe asked wearily. "Why not let them recover your dogs for you?"

Bennett shook his head. "Because what good are the damn dogs now? These idiots had their balls cut off! The dogs are good for nothing now! You have any idea how much I paid for all those dogs? You know how much it costs to feed them and vaccinate them every year? For what? So they walk around on tiptoes all prissy? Shit! They might as well have shot the damn dogs themselves."

There was a sound outside, but Zoe almost didn't hear it because Sam Bennett hadn't finished with his rant, even though she could no longer distinguish individual words. She tried to lever herself to her feet, but the next breath wouldn't come. Sitting back down with a thud, she saw Laurel still bent over the inert Dorsey, and Sam Bennett spewing ignorance like a geyser, and she watched in mild puzzlement as they slowly receded from her. For some reason, she could not draw a breath. She felt slight puzzlement, but no panic. The rifle stock slipped from her grip, and the weapon hit the floor.

Sam Bennett watched her fade and began to turn his back to her in order to grab the rifle with the hands bound behind his back.

Before he could, a barrage of uniformed police surged

through the doorway. Flashlights lit up the place like electricity had come to town, and drawn weapons all pointed toward Bennett as if they were compass needles and he the magnetic north. Had Zoe been aware enough to raise her head, she would have cheered.

Bennett collapsed back to his seated position, looking, except for the way his feet and hands fit so neatly together, very much like the sagging Zoe.

When Ruth and Ardell knocked at her door, Zoe had been home for two days. The soreness in her body was slowly turning to stiffness, and she was at a crossroads where the forced inactivity was both driving her crazy and a relief.

Zoe set aside the novel she had been reading and showed the sisters into what had once been the front parlor, a room no longer reserved just for company. The pocket doors opened to reveal a room sparsely, but comfortably, furnished, and showered in sunshine.

Ardell's hair was newly colored and styled. Ruth's was back in the bun. Both wore slacks with flowery pastel blouses tucked in beneath gray cardigans.

"We've been to see our lawyer," Ruth announced as soon as they were all settled. "She's already working on our defense strategy. Doesn't that have a ring to it? How are you feeling?"

"Better every day."

"There's a little something we would like to talk over with you, Zoe," Ardell said, casting a sidelong glance at Ruth.

"No mention's been made of that hidden room or the tunnel," Ruth said, leaning forward. "When the Ordinary was searched by the state police, no one found it. The sheriff has been nosing around, too, and I'm fairly certain he hasn't found it yet, but . . . we don't know what to do."

"Dismantle the still," Zoe said. "You've got to find another way of funding your work."

"Oh, the still's been taken down," Ardell nodded, declining to elaborate further. "But will the Underground Railroad still be able to operate?"

"You're not doing anything illegal."

"But if anyone goes disappearing in this county, Ethan McKenna might be getting a warrant to search us again. Don't you think?" Ruth pressed.

"I'm no more able to predict his actions than you are, but I'd say that as long as a woman has committed no crime, there's no reason to suspect her, and no reason anyone else would buy for issuing a warrant. If a woman wants to leave her husband, that's still no crime."

"And how about you?" Ruth asked coyly.

"Me?"

"Even if we somehow manage not to go to jail, we're going to be needing some help with the Railroad. We'd like to ask you to join us. We had Willa research your background, you know. It sounded to us as if the Underground Railroad would have come in handy had there been a stop near you in Washington, D.C." Ruth reached over and put a hand on Zoe's leg. "Maybe your friend could have been saved."

Instead of the rage and pain she usually touched in any memories of Karen, now Zoe felt a curious loosening in her chest. "Maybe she could have been," she said.

"Selling all our underground stock, if you know what I mean, and the addition of some money that started coming in after Willa wrote that nice story in the paper about the circumstances behind our arrest, have left us sitting kind of pretty. And, you'd be surprised at the number of former volunteers who have contacted us and told us they'd like to be more involved again. One or two of them were travelers themselves at one time.

"Anyway, we have arranged to have a third party talk to the owners of the property behind yours, in hopes that they will agree to sell. That house would make a fine station on the Railroad, don't you think? Once it's fixed up? We could rest the other one for a while, until the heat dies down. Or maybe even use them both. What do you think?"

"Yes," Zoe said, surprised to find herself blinking back tears. "It would be a fine idea if you could get that property. And it would be convenient for me to have it so close."

"That's just what we were hoping, dear," Ardell said, tapping the side of her nose. "That's just what we were hoping."

Several days later, after checking in with her own doctor, Zoe stopped at the hospital in answer to an invitation. Dorsey had been moved to a private room, and Laurel had told her he was coming along fine.

Goodness was recovering nicely at home. Two of Sam Bennett's hounds had survived his attack, and both would soon go to the new home Dorsey's friends had found for them.

Zoe knocked on the open door of Dorsey's room and walked in. Sitting beside the bed, Laurel stood up without letting go of Dorsey's hand. "You take this chair," Laurel directed. "You shouldn't be moving furniture and stuff."

To Dorsey, pale, but resting comfortably against the pillows and shining like a three-hundred-watt bulb, she added, "Remember I told you she had a collapsed lung? And, what, a couple of cracked ribs, Zoe? I don't think we would have made it out of that place without her, Dorsey."

Zoe, who still moved somewhat gingerly, slid into Laurel's vacated perch without dissension.

Then Zoe handed Laurel a package wrapped in tissue paper. It was a book about decorative and functional railings for porches and decks.

After all three exchanged reports of their conditions, Laurel told Zoe, "I wanted you to have a chance to talk to Susan."

"She's here?"

"She'll be calling in a few minutes. She wants to thank you. So do I."

"There's one thing I still don't understand," Zoe said, shifting a bit so she sat straighter. "When I first met you two, you were very secretive about Dorsey's identity. Now that Sam Bennett's been charged with Patrick Rourke's murder, and now that it's public knowledge that you mistakenly rescued Sam Bennett's dogs, assuming them to be Patrick Rourke's, what's left to hide?"

She wasn't sure she'd get an answer, but Zoe knew she'd probably never have a better opportunity to ask.

Laurel studied Dorsey's face, and his eyes sought hers. He pressed his lips together, and if possible, paled further.

"Revenuers," Laurel whispered when she turned back to Zoe.

"Alcohol, Tobacco, and Firearms?" Zoe asked. "But there's nothing outstanding—no warrants, not even an investigation, at least as far as I've been able to determine."

Her face clouded, Laurel clutched at Dorsey's hand. "No warrants? Not even for Tommy Jeffries?"

"Not even for him," Zoe confirmed.

"But, Dorsey, you told me the government agents were after you, or at least the state, and that you had to lay low—" Her voice trailed off.

The tip of Dorsey's tongue showed between his teeth. "I stole money," he said softly, his eyes flashing between Laurel and Zoe. "Are you sure there's no warrant out on me?"

"You told me it was running moonshine!" Laurel said, almost pleading for the more familiar scenario.

"There's no warrant," Zoe confirmed.

With a sigh, Dorsey said, "I lied about having the money for the license when we got married. I stole fifty bucks from the cash register at that pizza place where I was working. Mr. Dolores would have found out the next morning when he counted the money in the till. I figured he'd have the cops after me so fast—I wanted to marry Laurel, and I didn't want her to have to wait."

His eyebrows slid together, dangerously close to colliding. "Zoe, are you sure there's no warrant out for my arrest?"

"There's no warrant, Dorsey," Zoe assured him again.

"Why couldn't you just ask him for a loan?" Laurel demanded. "Or me? I'd have given you anything I had."

"I couldn't. I just couldn't. I'm sorry, honey. I couldn't even afford to pay for our blood tests, and there was that money just staring at me. So when I made out the deposit that night, I slipped the fifty into my pocket. It's been bothering me ever since. I kept thinking that I'd be arrested sooner or later, and I just didn't know how to tell you."

"You could have started with the truth," Laurel said, raising her chin. "We're married, Dorsey. You can't keep something like that from me."

"I'm sorry, Laurel. I'm so sorry! I'll pay him back!"

"We sure will! And write a letter of apology," Laurel added. "And we'll go there as soon as they let you out of here. And we'll do whatever we can to make things right with Mr. Dolores. And, Dorsey, no more lying to me."

He nodded morosely.

"Or stealing," Laurel added.

Silently, Dorsey nodded again.

"And next time you want to walk the deck or go up to the lookout room because you can't sleep for worry about whatever problem you have, you damn well better let me walk with you!" Laurel ordered, tucking Dorsey's hand to her chest, allowing the merest touch of a smile to flicker about her lips.

Laurel tucked her hair behind her ears with one hand, squeezed Dorsey's hand with the other, and told Zoe, "There's a story that goes with that double wedding ring quilt Susan had. My great-grandma's sister interlocked those wedding rings for a special reason. You want to hear it?"

"Another story about Taylors and their jewelry, huh?" Zoe felt a slow grin spread across her lips. "The quilt didn't originate in a poker game, did it?"

Laurel laughed, sharing a look with Dorsey. "There's no poker game in this story."

"Tell me."

And the phone began to ring.

Other Mysteries Available
from Spinsters Ink

Spinsters Ink was founded in 1978 to produce vital books for diverse women's communities. In 1986, we merged with Aunt Lute Books to become Spinsters/Aunt Lute. In 1990, the Aunt Lute Foundation became an independent nonprofit publishing program. In 1992, Spinsters moved to Minnesota.

Spinsters Ink publishes novels and nonfiction works that deal with significant issues in women's lives from a feminist perspective: books that not only name these crucial issues, but—more important—encourage change and growth. We are committed to publishing works by women writing from the periphery: fat women, Jewish women, lesbians, old women, poor women, rural women, women examining classism, women of color, women with disabilities, women who are writing books that help make the best in our lives more possible.

Spinsters titles are available at your local booksellers or by mail order through Spinsters Ink. A free catalog is available upon request. Please include $2.00 for the first title ordered and 50¢ for every title thereafter. Visa and Mastercard are accepted.

Spinsters Ink
32 E. First St., #330
Duluth, MN 55802-2002
USA

218-727-3222 (phone)   (fax) 218-727-3119
(e-mail) spinster@spinsters-ink.com
(website) http://www.spinsters-ink.com

Photo: Judy Pacasa

Trudy Labovitz lives near Beverage, West Virginia, and visits Zoe there often. *Ordinary Justice* is her first published novel.